ENEMY
WITHIN

PHILLIP
THOMPSON

SALVO PRESS
Bend, Oregon

This is a work of fiction.
All characters and events portrayed in this novel are
fictitious and not intended to represent real people
or places.

ENEMY WITHIN

Salvo Press
61149 South Hwy 97, Suite 134
Bend, OR 97702
www.salvopress.com

Cover Designed by Scott Schmidt

Library of Congress Catalog Card Number: 98-88362

ISBN: 0-9664520-2-X

Printed in Canada
First Edition

To Angie, the best influence I could ever have in my life

"We can no longer think of terrorists as malefactors who attack American interests abroad. The World Trade Center Bombing and Oklahoma City have destroyed that myth. Those who sponsor or support acts of terrorism are not beyond the reach of America's military might."

U.S. Secretary of Defense William S. Cohen
Council on Foreign Relations
New York, New York
September 14, 1998

Acknowledgments

This book could have not been made possible if I'd tried to write it by myself. There were so many along the way who contributed, even though some didn't realize they were doing so. Many people deserve my thanks and gratitude, and my hope is that I have not omitted anyone in the listing here.

Leading the list of people I'm indebted to is my mother, one of the strongest people I've ever known. She reared two children under the most adverse of circumstances without flinching, without a thought for herself. She was always there, with a word of encouragement or a firm swat on the behind. I can never repay her sacrifices, but I will never forget them.

Thanks also go to Scott Schmidt, a patient, caring editor who gave me a chance.

I'd also like to thank all those who believed, even—and especially—when I didn't: Scott Jerabek, who was there way back when, and helped me form characters during long nights at sea and on liberty; Buck and Marge Rogers, for their long-distance support and parental ear when I needed it and wanted it; Jill Stevens, simply because she cared; Chris and Carol Graff, who always had plenty of encouragement; Lisa Hodson and Lona Rice, because their faith wouldn't let me quit; Mark Singleton, a true warrior and true friend; B.J. Ramos, muse, friend, critic; Jeff Speights, the only one who knows where fact and fiction meet; and, finally, Neal and Stacey Noem, whose friendship transcends words.

Thanks also to the Marines who touched my life and, in doing so, influenced the characters of this book, especially Lt.Gen. H.C. Stackpole and Maj. Gen. Mike Myatt. Special thanks to Col. Bob MacPherson, the finest officer I ever knew—"There is no 'fear' in MacPherson."

A final word: Without two other women, none of this would have been possible. I was fortunate to have superb teachers who cared, who encouraged and who demanded. Barbara Pittman first showed me how to be creative. Pat Coffey pushed me to be creative. This book, ultimately, is the fruit of their labors.

PROLOGUE

C aptain Richard Hawkins, United States Marine Corps, slammed the telephone receiver back into its cradle.

"Shit!"

He reached across his desk and punched the intercom button. When a Marine answered, Hawkins leaned closer to the speaker.

"Sergeant Roberts, burn me off a copy of the standard answer we have for the survey," he ordered. "I just took another query about it."

Hawkins heard Sergeant Roberts chuckle under his breath.

"Aye, aye, sir," Roberts said. "I'll have it back to you in a few minutes."

Hawkins leaned back in his chair and rubbed his eyes. His anger passed as quickly as it had arisen, but the frustration he felt wouldn't go away.

The survey had become a major source of irritation for Hawkins, the public affairs officer at the Marine Corps Air Ground Combat Center, located near the town of Twentynine Palms in southern California's Mojave Desert.

Conducted four months earlier, the survey was the brainchild of a Naval Reserve lieutenant commander who was a student at the Naval Postgraduate School in Monterey, California. As part of his master's thesis, the subject of which was non-traditional roles of the military, such as humanitarian assistance and peacekeeping, the commander had devised a fifty-question survey which, supposedly, would gauge the feelings of active-duty military members on these roles, many of which were gaining popularity with the current Administration.

Most of the questions dealt with the military's role, United Nations command of U.S. troops, and the participation of the U.S. military in the U.N.

The last question, however, was the one that had caused so much frustration for Hawkins. This question asked the survey taker to consider a scenario in which the U.S. Congress had passed a law outlawing certain firearms. In the scenario, this law was enormously unpopular and had caused some groups to resist turning over their weapons. The closing statement of the scenario indicated that the President had ordered federal troops to confiscate weapons from these groups. The survey taker was then directed to indicate his level of agreement with the statement, "I would fire on American citizens who refused to relinquish their weapons."

The Naval officer selected Marine combat veterans as his test group. MCAGCC was a good source, as the units there had participated in Operation Desert Storm and had been to Somalia in 1992.

Unfortunately, or stupidly as Hawkins liked to think, the survey wasn't reviewed before it was distributed to the Marines. When the Naval officer contacted the MCAGCC Public Affairs Office, he was given permission by Hawkins' predecessor to conduct the survey, no questions asked.

Hawkins found it incredible that no one at MCAGCC had reviewed the survey, and his proof was in the storm of controversy that followed, when the survey was brought to the attention of a U.S. Congressman.

One survey participant had become so disturbed by the questions that he took an extra copy, which he forwarded to his Congressman.

Within days, the survey made the national news. The media gave it only moderate attention until some of the farther-leaning segments of society latched onto it. Soon, the situation was so distorted that MCAGCC was besieged with phone calls and letters demanding to know what the Marine Corps thought it was doing training people to confiscate weapons from Americans or shoot them in the attempt.

Hawkins had been the person who bore the brunt of these calls and letters. He had reviewed the situation from start to finish and had discussed the survey with the public affairs officer at Monterey. Hawkins hoped that eventually the controversy would fade away, but he still averaged three calls a week. Most of these calls he categorized as "kooks" from the lunatic fringe, but he took each one seriously.

He knew that many Americans had genuine concerns about the seemingly eroding freedoms in the United States. Hawkins himself thought the survey was ill-conceived and alarming with its questions about the right to keep and bear arms. Hawkins, along with just about every other Marine he knew, steadfastly believed in the Second Amendment, and had become more concerned about the direction the country seemed to be taking.

The door swung open and Sergeant Roberts swept through with a piece of paper in his hand. He set the paper on the desk in front of Captain Hawkins.

Glaring up at the smug smirk, Hawkins slowly signed the letter and handed it back to the sergeant.

"You know," Hawkins said, "I understand there's an opening at our embassy in Azerbaijan."

"What? And leave the Mojave Desert?" The sergeant left with the letter.

Hawkins leaned back in his chair and wondered if they might have an opening for a captain.

1

W ade Stuart crouched in the tall grass and absent-mindedly scratched a sand flea on his leg. He looked up at the velvet of the night sky and laughed to himself. It seemed absurd that he should be hunkered down in the grass next to Charlie Tanner. After all, they were on the middle of a barrier island twelve miles off the Mississippi coast, on a night which was, as Charlie had so eloquently put it, "darker than three feet up a bear's ass."

Yet, they squatted to avoid detection as they peered out at the black, warm water of the Gulf of Mexico.

He knew he could have handled the whole weapons shipment himself, but Tanner would have nothing to do with that. Every time there was work to be done, Tanner made damn sure he was in on it.

To make matters worse, Stuart felt Tanner's suspicion growing with each encounter. Even tonight, the man had glared at him more than once, his long, tanned arms folded over hands as tough as saddle leather.

He had returned the glare, but remained wary, watching Tanner closely, not trusting him enough to turn his back to him.

Tanner didn't say much as he crouched by Stuart, but his eyes were constantly roving, alert, and shining. When he was serious or concentrating, the overall impression was that of a large cat, spring-loaded and ready to pounce.

His unlikely partner grunted and pointed toward the sea. Stuart squinted, turned his head, and used his peripheral vision in the darkness. He didn't see anything.

The island was no more than a sand spit, less than a half mile long, and only a few hundred yards wide. It wasn't even named, nor was it on current maps. Stuart figured it didn't exist thirty years ago. Probably formed by Hurricane Camille. The tiny island was covered in scrub grass, about waist high, with a white sand skirt around a thatch of light green. Small enough to be overlooked in the daytime, but large enough to keep most boats away at night for fear of grounding, the island was perfect for tonight.

Seconds later, Stuart spied the incoming boat, just as Tanner went prone. He did the same, watching Tanner tug the binoculars out of the canvas bag that hung from his shoulder.

The only sound was the whisper of the small waves breaking on the soft sand.

Tanner glanced at his watch. "Yep. That's them," he said. "About ten minutes behind schedule, but still doing good. The pickup boats should be here in about an hour."

Stuart remained silent. He had laughed at the idea of smuggling weapons via boats when he first heard it. The methods used by Tanner had seemed juvenile, but after seeing it twice, he had to admit it worked.

He shook his head, still not really believing that military weapons were pouring into Mississippi and into the hands of some very dangerous men.

Tanner scrambled to his feet and met the boat at the water's edge. He talked with the skipper in a low voice.

Stuart could make out only fragments of the conversation drifting over the water and up the beach. Quiet laughter, friendly talk. The skipper casually swiveled his head every so often.

Stuart wondered if the skipper would be so comfortable if he knew that his head was in the night vision sights of six government-issue M16A2 rifles at this moment, rifles the skipper had delivered himself.

It was Stuart's task on these purchases to control the men aiming those rifles, men brought along as insurance in case of a double cross. He had been shocked when Tanner told him that the only firepower present in earlier transactions was a couple of revolvers, including one that Charlie Tanner kept in the back of his trousers.

Stuart had been adamant about beefing up the security here. Tanner had gone along with it, as long as Stuart would handle it and stay the hell in the weeds.

He agreed to that, and now realized that he had hamstrung himself with his flash of brilliance. He needed to see the skipper's face and learn his name, but Tanner insisted that he stay away from the boat on deliveries, arguing that the fewer faces seen, the better.

As Stuart watched the unloading and Tanner and the boat's skipper, he pulled a small camera, loaded with infrared film, from the front of his jeans and inched forward on his belly. He was far enough away from the other men in the bushes and the men on the beach so that the snapping of the shutter wouldn't be heard.

His vantage point gave him an excellent angle to get shots of Tanner and the skipper and the growing stack of weapons crates.

He started snapping pictures: three of the crates, a couple of the skipper's men unloading them, and a few of the boat. The rest of the roll was devoted to Tanner and the skipper supervising at the water's edge. Stuart rewound the roll, popped it out of the camera, and stashed it in the pocket of the windbreaker he wore. The camera went back into the front of his trousers.

When the unloading was complete, the skipper quickly wrapped up his conversation as Tanner walked back to his hiding spot. Stuart handed up Tanner's briefcase. Tanner returned, paid the skipper, and stood patiently as the skipper opened the case to count the money.

The skipper yanked a flashlight out of his back pocket and started counting the money, giving Stuart his first view of the man's features. Broad face, flat nose. Medium mouth, dark tan.

Almost a friendly-looking old-salt-of-the-sea type. His hair was long, and either gray or blond.

The skipper snapped the case shut, stuffed the light back into his pocket, and shook hands with Tanner. He clambered aboard his boat and immediately shoved off into the darkness.

Tanner shuffled up to Stuart. "Well, shouldn't be long now," he said.

Stuart glanced at his watch, and nodded. "That the same guy as last time?"

"Yeah. Why?"

"Just wondering. Didn't seem like the same man. He talked a lot tonight."

"Guess he felt friendly or something. Why?" Tanner asked.

"I just said he talked a lot, that's all. Anything interesting?"

"Same old shit."

Stuart tried another approach. "How long does it take him to make it out here?" He could feel Tanner's glare in the night.

"Shit, I don't know," Tanner said. "As long as it takes. He's always on time. What difference does it make?"

"Just making conversation," Stuart said. "What the hell else is there to talk about? I was just sitting here looking at the boat. It's a pretty good size, has a decent range, and probably has an engine that would surprise you. I was just kind of curious about how fast he could get out here and back. Where does this guy come from, anyway?"

"How should I know?" Tanner said. "I just see him when he gets here, and I don't ask no questions. You'd be smart to do the same."

Stuart shrugged. "Come on, Charlie. Don't be an asshole."

Tanner leaped forward until he was nose to nose with Stuart. "Who are you calling an asshole?"

Stuart raised a hand. His peripheral vision detected movement to his left. "Take it easy. I didn't mean anything."

"Fuck you, Stuart," Tanner hissed. "I don't need any smartass comments from you."

He stared calmly into Tanner's angry face. To Stuart's left, two men appeared. One was taller than Stuart and about forty pounds overweight. Apparently, the man was unable to find a T-shirt to fit him, as the one he wore left his huge belly exposed. The other man was about Stuart's height, but his frame was far more fragile.

He didn't know their names. To him, they were another pair of sullen rednecks. They had been on all the weapons purchases with Stuart, and he had taken to thinking of the two, who seemed inseparable, as "Fatman and Little Boy."

Neither held a weapon and neither, Stuart thought, appeared interested in conversation. The men had rarely said a word to him, except for an occasional derisive snort or snide remark about "some Marine Corps hotshot trying to teach country boys how to shoot."

He stepped toward them, then stopped about eight feet away. Fatman and Little Boy settled into the sand and eyed him. Little Boy grinned, his missing eye tooth a seemless void back through an empty brain.

"Evening, boys," Stuart said. Although he wasn't sure what they wanted, his body was tensed, ready to react if trouble came.

Fatman grunted, his belly jiggling over his belt.

Little Boy just stood there with his gap-toothed grin.

"What's on your mind?" Stuart asked. He noticed that Tanner had disappeared from the beach. Stuart knew the two men were going to try to take him, although he couldn't fathom a reason why. He knew that, with men like these, the reason never mattered much. His only question was, which one was carrying the knife he knew had to be there.

"Well," Little Boy finally said, "we was just wonderin,' since you know so much about weapons and fighting from when you was in the Marine Corps, how much did you learn about hand-to-hand fighting?"

Fatman grunted again, this time as if he was amused.

"I learned some," Stuart replied slowly, looking Little Boy in the eyes. "Why? Are you interested in learning some?"

The smaller man chortled through his missing tooth. "Yep, we sure are. Maybe you could teach us some."

Stuart shifted his weight slightly onto his left foot. He figured Little Boy, being smaller and more agile, would be the first in his range, so he focused his concentration on the spot where he calculated Little Boy's chin would be when he struck.

"Sure," Stuart said. "We could set something up."

"How about right now?"

"Well, I'm busy right now, but maybe tomorrow," Stuart said.

Little Boy took a step toward Stuart. "Now," he said. "Right goddamn now." He lunged toward him.

Having calculated the point of impact perfectly, Stuart shifted his weight to the left, let Little Boy slip almost past him before snapping his right arm out and forward. Swinging like an ax blade, his hand caught Little Boy just under the chin with the force of a baseball bat, and the smaller man landed squarely on his back.

Gasping, Little Boy rolled to one side clutching his throat.

Stuart swiveled around toward Fatman, who glowered from a crouch. Stuart feinted with his head to the right, then spun completely around on his left foot. As he came around, his booted right foot smashed against the right side of Fatman's head.

The spinning kick was so quick that it froze Fatman in place. The blow glanced off his skull, caught his nose, breaking it, and the fat man crumpled to the sand.

Then Stuart pivoted to his right to face Little Boy, who had shakily regained his feet, with a knife in his right hand. Wheezing at Stuart, he charged unsteadily. Stuart sidestepped him and lashed his right foot out and down. He smashed Little Boy's right knee, doubling him over in agony. With little effort but crushing force, Stuart punched him squarely on the chin and sent him to the ground, unconscious.

Still in a crouch, Stuart let out his breath. He glanced around the area nervously as the adrenaline wore off. He saw no one, and wondered where Tanner had gone. He gulped the cool air to steady his nerves.

Suddenly, Tanner burst from the scrub brush. "What the hell's going on?"

Stuart stared at him. "Where the hell have you been?"

Tanner shrugged. "I went to check on things, then I heard all this ruckus. What the hell did you do to these guys?"

He shook his head as he realized that Tanner had set the fight up. "Just giving 'em some lessons in self-defense."

Just then the pick up boats came ashore.

"I'm going to get everybody loaded up," Stuart said. As he walked away, he could feel Tanner's eyes on his back.

Walking down the beach to watch the weapons get loaded onto a boat, Stuart approached the craft. It was a new Cigarette. Steel-blue, gorgeous and perfect for smuggling. After all, it was originally designed to smuggle cigarettes, so why not use it to smuggle guns?

Stuart leaned casually against the bow, as if supervising the men straining to get the weapons on board. Three hundred M16A2 military rifles packed in wooden crates could get cumbersome. He carefully memorized the registration number of the boat stenciled on the bow.

The Cigarette sped away as soon as the weapons were loaded, and Stuart had the crew check the island for loose gear which may have been dropped. He stayed on the beach for a moment gazing at the dark Gulf. He was pleased he was able to get the registration number from at least one of the boats. And the photographs. But that was a lot of rifles, he thought.

2

Next morning, Special Agent Wade Stuart of the Bureau of Alcohol, Tobacco and Firearms rolled out of bed and rubbed his eyes, immediately alert, although he had been asleep scarcely three hours. It was a trait he'd learned years ago. He snatched the heavy motel room curtain across the windows and blinked. Already hot outside.

He frowned at the disheveled pile of college textbooks and file folders on the furniture and the male debris of weeks of one-room living, caused by the collision of his three lives: student, federal agent and militia lieutenant.

Since coming to Bedford, a sleepy hamlet tucked into the hills of northern Mississippi, Stuart hadn't devoted much time to housekeeping. He had split his time between the activities of the Mississippi People's Militia—of which he was a new member—and maintaining his cover as a graduate student at the University of Mississippi, a half-hour's drive west of Bedford.

When he had arrived in town a few weeks earlier to investigate rumors about a gun-smuggling operation, Stuart had not even been sure the militia existed.

Ever since, he had been overwhelmed.

The militia's leader, a seventy-seven-year-old retired farmer named Amos Moreland, had, along with the county sheriff, Thomas Gage, set up an apparatus which brought weapons into the state to arm the growing number of members of the Mississippi People's Militia and other groups.

And since bringing Stuart on board, Moreland and Gage had picked his brain for ways to train the militiamen and improve the MPM compound deep in the woods of Bedford's Junkin County. Which was why it had taken him a few weeks to get around to renting an apartment, he griped to himself as he dressed and began transferring the clutter of his room to his car.

He drove to the Magnolia Heights apartment complex. The name made Stuart laugh when he wheeled the car into the parking lot and surveyed the area. The two-story brick building was surrounded by pines and oaks and was situated on level ground.

He went to the manager's office and met a young woman who introduced herself as Lee Ann, the resident manager. She fished around in the pockets of her oversized trousers for a key, shoved her brown hair away from her face, then showed Stuart the furnished one-bedroom flat on the second floor. Stuart inspected the room swiftly but expertly, bringing to Lee Ann's attention a bedroom window that wouldn't open and a leaky bathroom faucet, which she agreed to have repaired. Stuart followed Lee Ann back to her office to sign the lease and pay the security deposit and one month's rent.

Minutes later, Stuart removed a laptop computer from under one arm and a bag of groceries from under the other. He yanked a bottle of water from the bag as he shoved the groceries into the refrigerator. He walked into his bedroom and put his computer on the bureau.

After about two minutes, his e-mail screen appeared and Stuart saw that he had no new messages. Somewhat disappointed, he typed in a brief message to Raymond Carr, the Assistant Director of the ATF, and explained his movements over the last six days, then transmitted it.

On the return trip from Wal-Mart to purchase necessities, Stuart drove through the outskirts of Bedford, a town of about ten thousand souls, past the motels, fast-food restaurants, billboards and neon lights one expected to see anywhere in America. He passed yet another one of the seemingly millions of garish mini-marts that were now spreading through the South like kudzu. He had always felt that kudzu was a damn sight more pleasing to the eye than the raw neon and chrome of the mini-mart.

After unloading his cleaning gear, Stuart decided an hour's worth of exercise in the Magnolia Heights pool would do him some good. He donned swimming trunks and found the sidewalk that led to the pool behind the apartment building.

The first thing he noticed was a woman lying serenely on a plastic lounge chair; a striking brunette in a rather small white bikini. Only by staring did Stuart realize that this was the resident manager he'd met only hours earlier. He had mistakenly guessed earlier that she was a dowdy teenager.

He could now see that she was not. Maybe in her early twenties, but certainly not a teenager. The usual softness of pubescent baby fat was absent, replaced by a solid leanness that Stuart found instantly arousing. She had long, strong legs, tapered muscles, excellently formed hips, flat belly, and a deep brown tan that gave her a healthy, somehow feline, quality. Her face, partially shielded by sunglasses, was as healthy-looking as her body, tanned, taut, and unadorned by cosmetics. Her hair spilled across her forehead and shoulders.

Stuart suddenly felt conspicuous and willed his legs to move. Since there were no other swimmers present, he walked to the empty chair next to the girl.

She smiled brightly. "Hey," she said, in a voice totally different from that of the resident manager. Just as accented, but not nearly as juvenile.

Stuart returned her greeting and asked permission to sit.

"Sure," she said, much to Stuart's relief. "I was about bored out of my skull." She took off her sunglasses, widened her green eyes, and took on a conspiratorial look. "I'm not really supposed to be here while I'm working. You won't tell, will you?"

Stuart laughed. "Are you kidding? No, I won't tell."

She looked relieved. "Good." She sat up. "I'm Lee Ann

Weatherby."

"Wade Stuart."

"Yes, I remember," she said. "Welcome to Magnolia Heights. Are you new to Bedford?"

"Yeah, I just moved here in time for the fall semester at Ole Miss," Stuart said, hoping he wasn't gawking too badly.

"You're a student?"

He nodded. "First year grad student. International relations."

Lee Ann was a local, about to begin her third year at Ole Miss. She was a communicative disorders major, which impressed Stuart. She was twenty-three and a member of Delta Gamma sorority, but only because it was impossible to have any kind of decent social life if you weren't in a sorority. Stuart smiled to himself, thinking of his days as an undergraduate student at Ole Miss, when he had thought the same thing, although he had never been able to afford fraternity dues.

When Lee Ann asked Stuart about himself, he answered cautiously. He told her he was originally from Biloxi, which wasn't true. She noted the year he said he graduated and asked, "So, what have you been doing for the last few years?"

"I was in the Marine Corps after I graduated," Stuart said carefully, wondering how she would react.

Lee Ann's eyebrows popped above her sunglasses. "Really? That must have been interesting. What did you do?"

He looked at her closely. He was accustomed to people feigning interest in his military service, only to look away, bored, when he began talking about it. Her interest, however, seemed real.

"Actually," he said, "it wasn't very interesting. I was in the infantry. A lot of walking, being dirty, and sleeping in the mud."

She dismissed him with a wave. "Oh, I bet it wasn't so bad. Did you get to see the world?"

"Some of it," replied Stuart. He briefly described the countries he had visited.

When he mentioned Rome, she sat up straight. "Rome?" she

said. "I've always wanted to go there. Tell me all about it."

Hours passed as they chatted, pausing frequently to swim. When Lee Ann asked him what had brought him to Bedford, he explained that his car had broken down on the way to Ole Miss, and while waiting for it to be repaired, he'd found the apartment and decided to live in Bedford and commute to school.

Early in the afternoon, Stuart asked, "What exactly is there to do in this town?"

Lee Ann, climbing out of the pool, shook the water from her hair, and said, "Like I told you, not much. Hey, the fair is in town this week."

"Really? That might be worthwhile. I used to love the fair when I was a kid, and I haven't been to one in years."

Lee Ann sat beside him, crossed her legs, and leaned back, supporting herself with her arms. He wondered if she did it intentionally. "Well, you want to go?" she said.

"That's a great idea. What time?"

Lee Ann stood and collected her things. "About seven?"

"Fine." Stuart stretched out on the chair, basking in the sun's glare.

Lee Ann told him she lived in the same building, Apartment 38B. "See you tonight," she called over her shoulder as she left.

He studied her as she walked off.

As Stuart and Lee Ann walked toward the gate to the fairgrounds, he felt a familiar excitement. He remembered the days from his boyhood when the fair was in town, and its exotic possibilities drew youngsters from across the county.

"Ladies and Gentlemen," the man would say, drawing out each word dramatically. "Feast your eyes on a truly remarkable twist of nature! See the half woman/half tiger raised deep in the jungles of India! She's ferocious! Untamed! Step inside!"

In his mind, Stuart could see the trapeze artists spinning and tumbling, the strong men bending horseshoes with their bare hands, the games and chances to win, and the glittering neon lights of scores of seemingly death-defying, hair-raising rides. As a boy, Stuart had eagerly awaited the arrival of the convoy of trucks that brought the fair to town. He would read the billboards and posters daily, counting the hours until his parents would take him inside the swirling frenzy of activity. For this one night, he could gorge himself on sweets and stay up late.

Stuart smiled wistfully as he and Lee Ann purchased ten dollars worth of tickets for the rides inside the chain link fence surrounding the fairgrounds.

As he and Lee Ann walked through the turnstile, he was assaulted by the mix of aromas of the carnival: the sharp smell of hot popcorn, the sickeningly sweet smell of cotton candy. A permeating whiff of hot dogs and hamburgers. They stood, undecided for a moment, in front of a high school band boosters pavilion.

"Where do you want to start?" Lee Ann asked.

"I don't know," he replied, then quickly remembered a lesson from his childhood. "But we better get on the rides before we eat."

Lee Ann laughed heartily. He liked the sound of it.

They took on all the daring rides with an utter disdain for danger: the Scrambler, the Zipper, the roller coaster, and others, even the Tilt-A-Whirl. It occurred to him that this was the most fun he had had in a long while.

Several times, she linked her arm in his and hung on tightly, squealing with delight as they were spun round and round, up and down, by long-haired, seedy ride operators.

After the rides, they had hot dogs and a beer. When he stepped away from the counter with their second round of beer, he saw Charlie Tanner, about forty feet behind Lee Ann.

Stuart felt Lee Ann staring at him. She turned and peered at the man, then quickly turned back to Stuart.

"Damn," she said. "Are you looking at that tall skinny guy back there?"

"Huh? Oh, yeah, I guess so," Stuart said. Tanner disappeared into the dark crowd of moving people. "Do you know him?"

"Yes," she said, sighing. "He asked me out a few times, but I never would go."

"Why not?"

She glanced at him curiously, then laughed. "He's not my type."

"This isn't going to cause a scene, is it? I mean, he seemed to be staring pretty hard."

"No, I don't think so," she said. "He's probably just mad. Are you going to offer me one of those beers, or what?"

They sipped their drinks as they slowly walked among the game tables. When they got to the shooting gallery, Stuart couldn't resist. He picked up the pellet pistol, smiled at Lee Ann, and then took aim at the moving tin ducks. He dropped four ducks in rapid succession.

She swiveled her head at him, then at the ducks, then at Stuart again. She smiled.

The booth operator scowled at Stuart. "All right, Mac, you're a winner," he said reluctantly. "What'll it be?"

Stuart looked at Lee Ann, and she pointed at a four-foot teddy bear. The hawker pulled it down and handed it over.

She laughed merrily. "Do it again."

Stuart shrugged and passed the hawker another dollar bill. He took the pistol, drew a breath, let out half, just like he had been taught. He squeezed the trigger four times, and again four ducks dropped from sight.

Lee Ann squealed with delight. "I get another one."

"Okay, pal, two's the limit," the hawker grumbled.

Stuart looked at Lee Ann again, but she said, "You choose this time."

Stuart asked for the first stuffed animal he saw, a lion, and handed it to Lee Ann, who grinned. He thanked the man in the booth and they moved on.

It was a tight fit on the Ferris wheel, with the two of them plus the trophies. Lee Ann chatted, telling Stuart that she couldn't believe he won two times, especially when nobody ever wins at the fair, and, anyway, how did he learn to shoot so well?

The slow ride was almost hypnotic, and as they reached the top of the wheel, the cool air was a welcome respite from the swelter below. She wrapped her arm around his and lay her head on his shoulder. She yawned, and for a second he thought she had fallen asleep. But, she sat up, and said, "This has been fun. I'm glad you conned me into asking you out."

"Lee Ann," he said. "Honestly, I didn't—"

"Oh, shut up," she said, and smiled. "I was kidding. I couldn't care less, and I've had a good time."

As the Ferris wheel spun downward, Stuart noticed Tanner again, sipping a beer and glaring up at him. When the wheel came around again, Tanner was gone. What the hell was he doing there, Stuart wondered.

Later, walking back to the car, Lee Ann said, "Did you see all those kids looking at me with my two big ol' stuffed animals? I bet they were so jealous." She seemed to take great joy in it.

He chuckled quietly. He held the animals as Lee Ann dug her keys out of the pocket of her jeans. He was idly staring back at the fair when he felt her step closer to him. He turned and bumped against her, surprised that she was so close.

She looked up at him, then lay a soft hand on his cheek and kissed him. He felt her lips, warm and full, and her curious tongue. He returned her kiss and found himself pushing her against the car. He could feel her breasts crushed against him, and then felt silly holding two stuffed animals in his arms while he kissed her. He stepped back slowly to catch his breath.

Lee Ann studied him sheepishly. Her face, lit by the splash of neon behind them, was flushed, and she was breathing rapidly. She gave a small smile, and then burst into laughter. He laughed also, shaking his head.

"How romantic," she said, as she unlocked the door and slid into the car. Stuart followed her, throwing the animals into the back seat. Still laughing, Lee Ann threw her hair back, started the car, and they drove away from the fair.

He glanced around behind them, searching for Tanner again, but he was nowhere to be seen.

After they kissed again at Lee Ann's apartment, he promised her he'd take her on a real date. Then he walked to his apartment, fell into his bed, and lay there for a long while, conflicted with his feelings and unsure about why Tanner had followed him at the fair.

3

Early the next morning, after his morning run, Stuart drove downtown to the sheriff's office. An air conditioner appeared to be in operation, but it must have been a weak one, as the temperature inside the Sheriff's Department was scarcely five degrees cooler than the outside air.

Stuart surveyed his surroundings. He stood in a long, dingy corridor painted a sickly green.

To his right was a window covered in Plexiglas, with a circle of holes for speaking through. He squinted and peered into the darkness opposite the barrier. No one. He turned and strode down the corridor until he saw a sign over the top of a dark wooden door which read, simply, "Sheriff."

He hesitated, his knuckles wavering over the surface of the door. He heard nothing. He rapped on the door solidly.

"Come in," Sheriff Thomas Gage barked from inside the office.

Stuart reluctantly stepped inside, his eyes scanning the room quickly before coming to rest on Gage, who sat behind his desk over a sheaf of what appeared to be computer paper, although no computer was evident. To his right was Amos Moreland sitting back in a corner of a leather couch with a smug look.

The sheriff's office reflected his personality—rough, tough, and somewhat arrogant. It had the only window in the outer area separating the jail cells in the rear from the office spaces. The brick walls were painted light brown. His desk was large and cluttered. A green blotter covered most of the top, and had phone numbers and names scribbled across it.

On the wall behind the desk, mounted in a large black frame, was Gage's honorable discharge from the Army. The document was the centerpiece of Gage's display, as it was centered over his chair. Surrounding the discharge were other certificates of achievement collected over his terms as sheriff.

On the opposite wall were several photos of Gage: two black and whites of Sergeant Gage in his Army uniform in Vietnam; one color eight-by-ten of his swearing-in ceremony when he was elected sheriff; and others showing Gage shaking hands with various people.

"Good morning, sheriff," Stuart said.

"Morning," Gage replied.

"Morning, Wade," Moreland said.

Stuart returned the greeting and nodded at Gage as the sheriff went to the corner of the office to draw a cup of coffee.

"Tom, you ought to be the one to tell Wade how we go about transferring our purchases," Moreland said as Gage handed Stuart a steaming Styrofoam cup.

Gage told Stuart that now that the weapons had been bought, brought into the state, and the Mississippi People Militia's cut taken out, Stuart would drive south to Electric Mills, a tiny logging hamlet in the Piney Woods region of Mississippi, with the remaining one hundred rifles to make another deal.

Moreland gestured at Stuart, who sat on the sheriff's leather couch beside him.

"You and Charlie will go down there with the rifles," Gage said. Y'all will be in a green pickup with Mississippi plates. There'll be a tarp over the bed. When you get down to Electric Mills, Charlie will show the road to take. It's an old dirt road the pulpwood trucks used to use, but it's abandoned now.

"Anyhow, he'll show you," Gage continued. "When the contact comes, he'll go past you until he's out of sight. That's when you and Charlie will check to see if he was followed. Charlie will show you how. If everything's ready, just sit tight. Our man will back up to you."

"How does he know it's clear?" Stuart asked.

"Pre-arranged signal. See, the road's so narrow that you and Charlie will have to be off in the woods to let the contact pass by. That also means that if he's being followed, the tail will have to go right past you—you're going to be hidden. If he's being followed, you just wait a few minutes and ease on out of there without getting caught by whoever may be tailing our buyer. Then we just set up another buy with our contact."

"Wait," Stuart said. "What are we supposed to do with the weapons? If we get caught with them, we're fucked. If we leave them, the contact could pick them up without paying us and we'd still be fucked."

Gage's brow furrowed. Moreland seemed uninterested. Then Gage smiled. "Never happen," he said. "The whole point, if our buyer is being followed, which ain't likely, is to wait until they're both out of sight. Nobody but you and Charlie know anything about where the weapons are. Hell, the way these weapons are brought in off the Coast, nobody could figure out all the possible moves we could make."

Stuart thought the system was amateurish, and not foolproof, but he wasn't about to tell Gage that.

Moreland looked at Stuart and asked, "Anything else?"

Stuart glared back at Moreland. "You explained how you buy these weapons," he said. "And now you've explained how you distribute them to different people, but without making much profit off the resale. What I want to know is why all the trouble to set up an organization to sell weapons if all you want to do is arm the MPM?"

Moreland smiled. "We ain't in this thing for money," he said. "Sure, we have to make a little to make the whole thing work, but we're not interested in the profit. We're trying to get as many weapons as possible to the people who need them."

"Those people being other militias?" Stuart said.

"Yes," Moreland said. "Or anybody who's organized for and

supports the principles of freedom. Don't you see? We're mobilizing. This is only the first part. Once all the groups are armed, we'll be ready to take back what's ours."

Stuart gazed at Gage, who was nodding seriously at Moreland's every sentence.

"That's why we need your skills," Moreland said. "We're moving entirely too slowly right now. We need to get bigger shipments, step up the distribution, begin training. And if you're as good as you say you are, then you can definitely help us out."

"That's right," Gage said. "When you came into town a few weeks ago asking about a militia, I thought all my prayers had been answered. Hell, who wouldn't want a Marine infantry officer training their militia?"

Stuart smiled. "Oh, I can help you out," he said. "Training won't be difficult, if we can get the money to do it right."

"We'll get the money," Moreland said. "We've come too far already to stop."

Stuart glanced at his watch. It was almost noon. He announced that he was going to get lunch.

Moreland rose with him and said, "Wade, I'm serious when I say that I'm glad to have you on our side. If you see any room for improvement, just let me know."

"Don't worry," Stuart said. "I will."

That night Stuart picked Lee Ann up at her apartment promptly at six-thirty. She was dressed simply in a skirt and blouse, but looked beautiful nonetheless. They went to the local twin cinema for a movie, in which Stuart was only half interested. Afterwards, they stopped for dinner. Nothing fancy, just steaks at a quiet restaurant on the outskirts of town. The conversation was light and trivial, both asking polite questions about the other. Stuart felt more relaxed than he had in months.

As he sipped black coffee after dinner, Lee Ann leaned forward and looked directly into Stuart's eyes. "Wade," she said in a low voice, "let's leave."

In his apartment, he offered Lee Ann a beer. He settled onto the couch beside her and, not knowing what else to do, asked her if she wanted to watch television.

She smiled at him. It made him slightly uncomfortable. "Drink your beer," he said.

Her face was serious, but her eyes were shining. She leaned over and slowly wrapped her arms around his neck. In a sultry voice she said, "Later." She kissed him, looked into his eyes and smiled. "After."

Stuart looked back into her green eyes; he saw that her cheeks were flushed. He quickly took her in his arms. They lunged at each other, falling against the sofa. He kissed her hard and strong, and she responded passionately. They parted just as suddenly, each panting with desire. Neither spoke a word as they walked to his bedroom.

Stuart drew the back of his left hand slowly across his forehead, wiping beads of perspiration from his brow. His right hand rested under his head, propped up against a pillow. He stared at the ceiling. Lee Ann nestled beside him. He turned his head slightly, trying not to wake her.

She was curled up in the fetal position, hands tucked under her chin, forehead pressed against his chest.

Even in the darkness, he could see the contented look on her face. The moonlight that seeped in from a crack in the curtains bathed her in a peaceful blue light that shone on her nude flank.

He admired her for a moment, then looked back at the ceiling and smiled, but not smugly. Their pace had been furious, almost demanding, although he had taken his time in order to fully enjoy the encounter. These thoughts amused him and he laughed softly to himself.

The noise woke Lee Ann, who murmured a sleepy "Hmmm?" then rolled onto her belly. One eye opened and peered for a moment of comprehension at Stuart. Then she smiled in contentment.

"Sorry," he said, "didn't mean to wake you."

She yawned and pulled herself onto his chest. He could feel her breasts pressing against him. "So," she said, now fully coherent. "What are you going to do tomorrow? Or is it today?"

Stuart glanced at the luminous dial of the watch resting on the nightstand. "Today." He put his hand on the small of her back, then let it slide downward. "Nothing much. Why?"

"My uncle is having a party at his house tomorrow afternoon—this afternoon. Would you like to come?"

"A party?" he said.

"Yeah. My uncle—actually, he's my great-uncle—throws a big barbecue every summer in his backyard, and invites lots of people."

Stuart thought it over. Lots of people? He might be able to pick up some loose ends of conversations. Besides, it would be a decent meal, an afternoon with Lee Ann, and time away from his investigation.

"Sure. Why not?"

"That'd be great," Lee Ann said. "We'll leave about ten o'clock?"

She smiled and closed her eyes and they both drifted back to sleep.

4

The doorbell roused Stuart from his sleep. He shook his head clear, then heaved himself up from his comfortable position and squinted at his clock; 0922. He climbed out of bed and searched for his clothes, only then realizing that he was alone. He found his shorts under the bed, then grabbed half a dozen beer bottles and deposited them in the wastebasket in the kitchen. He saw a note on the table. Lee Ann's note explained that she had to "get ready for the BBQ."

He walked to the front door and snatched it open.

"Boy, somebody looks like he was up all night," Lee Ann said.

Stuart wondered if she had intended the play on words. Her expression meant she did. He laughed and asked her in while he dressed.

During the drive to her uncle's house, Lee Ann talked of her impending return to school in the fall and how she was looking forward to it. Stuart limited himself mostly to polite responses, but occasionally carried his share of the conversation.

About ten miles down the road, Lee Ann slowed, then turned right onto a gravel road lined with trees. The road was long and relatively straight, and eventually opened into a vast open area in the middle of a thick pine forest. Stuart was taken aback at what he saw. It was an enormous home—obviously an antebellum plantation house, two stories topped by a round cupola with windows all around.

The exterior was a blinding white. Four ornate columns

reached magnificently to the second floor. The front porch steps led down to a wide brick walkway that extended for what seemed like half an acre, through rows of massive magnolias. Stuart shook his head, amazed.

Lee Ann drove to the side of the house and parked. Stuart, still in shock, forced himself out of the car and faced the eight-foot high wall of shrubbery that apparently bordered the back yard. He could hear sounds of the party and could smell the tangy scent of barbecued pork.

Lee Ann took his arm and led him inside, into the back yard. Nearly a hundred people milled casually about, chatting amiably, sipping alcoholic beverages. Stuart could see three kegs of beer at a bar, which was tended expertly by a silver-haired gentleman.

The barbecue was being conducted in the far corner of the yard; Stuart could see the spit turning slowly. Long tables with linen tablecloths held mountains of food.

He noticed that most of the people carried the look of money— cool, aloof, well-tailored. He felt conspicuous in khaki trousers and a loose-fitting green T-shirt. A hand slipped a glass in his. He murmured his thanks, and sipped the beer. He looked at Lee Ann, who was perfectly at ease. It was obvious she was accustomed to this.

Lee Ann stood on her toes and furrowed her brow, searching the crowd. Stuart glanced at her with a questioning look, and she explained that she was looking for her uncle so he could meet him. She found him soon enough.

Squeezing his hand, she towed him through the crowd toward the tables. Along the way, several people recognized her and greeted her politely. Stuart only gaped, hoping he didn't look too ridiculous.

When Lee Ann stopped abruptly, Stuart almost spilled his beer down her back. He was looking to the right, trying to determine if anyone had seen his near-blunder, when he heard Lee Ann's voice.

"Hello, Uncle Amos. There's someone I want you to meet,"

Lee Ann said.

Stuart turned his head slowly and looked into the smiling face of Amos Moreland.

He wondered if his anxiety was evident as he stared into Moreland's face. He fought to maintain his composure. Moreland smiled warmly at his niece and Stuart. But when he looked at Stuart, there was something hard—dangerous—behind his eyes. A thousand alarm bells clanged in Stuart's head. His first impulse was that he had been set up, lured into Moreland's turf by Lee Ann. He immediately regretted the thought and cursed himself for being stupid and paranoid. It was pure coincidence. But if it was, why the hard look from Moreland?

Stuart noticed his glass was empty just in time to hear Moreland ask him, "Lee Ann says you've rented an apartment here in town?" Stuart noticed that she had slipped away. He took another beer from a passing tray, then turned back to Moreland and decided to play along.

"Yessir, that's right."

"Well, Bedford is a good quiet place to study." Moreland smiled that same warm smile—only this time Stuart saw that it was devoid of emotion.

"Yessir," he replied, more casually than he felt. "That's what I thought, too."

Stuart slowly turned his head to face Moreland. The old man was no longer smiling.

"Wade," Moreland said in a low voice, "why don't we go inside and talk for a few minutes. There's a few...issues we need to discuss."

"Sure," Stuart said warily. What the hell was Moreland up to? Stuart knew that he was in dangerous territory, that it was quite possible that Moreland knew everything about him somehow and was laying a not-too-well-disguised trap. He fought down the panic. All he could do was go along with it for now.

"Come on into the house," Moreland said.

Stuart took a last glance around for Lee Ann, then dutifully followed Moreland across the lawn and up the white steps of the broad back porch.

Moreland led him down a long hall decorated with expensive rugs and ornate mirrors. He turned into a room that was obviously a study. As Stuart entered, staring at his surroundings, Moreland closed the door.

In the den, Moreland offered Stuart a drink. He nodded and said, "Whiskey and water."

Moreland smiled and pulled a bottle of Wild Turkey from a shelf by his desk and splashed two inches of liquor into a tumbler, followed by a quarter-inch of water. Moreland handed the drink to Stuart.

"Have a seat, Wade."

Moreland gestured toward a comfortable-looking, and expensive-looking, couch. Stuart accepted the drink and took a seat.

He looked at his surroundings. Impressive, he thought. Money, lots of it. Huge polished mahogany desk adorned with the obligatory green blotter, heavy glass paperweight, and two wooden "in/out" boxes.

Against one wall, shelves filled with books almost reached the ceiling. Stuart noticed a couple of titles dealing with modern agriculture.

Moreland didn't sit beside Stuart; he returned to his desk, sitting regally in his high-back leather chair. A very important-looking chair, Stuart thought.

The two men exchanged pleasantries about the weather for a few moments, then Moreland came to the point.

"Wade, I've done some research on you over the last couple of weeks, and I must admit that I'm really impressed with your credentials."

Stuart was terrified that Moreland might know his real identity. He looked at Moreland until he realized that a response was expected, though he had no idea what that response was supposed to be. "Yessir," he said lamely.

"Wade, I'm going to cut right to the chase," Moreland began.

"I like you. And I think you might be the answer to a few of my current problems. You've been in a few scrapes and handled yourself pretty well. Am I right?"

"Yes, I suppose it is," Stuart said. He didn't want to get into what Moreland was alluding to, which he presumed was his combat experience.

"I thought so." Moreland smiled. "Our organization is small at the moment, but it grows every day that idiot president of ours is in the White House. And it will continue to grow, especially as more and more people come to their senses. But, we have another thing working in our favor, and that is you. You can help us reach our ultimate goal." Moreland's face flickered with the same emotionless smile as before.

"What exactly is that goal?" Stuart asked. "I've already agreed to train the militia—as long as we negotiate a price."

"We'll talk about money in a minute," Moreland said. "The goal is to take back control of the country, by first taking back control of our state."

"And how might you do that?"

"Very simple," Moreland said. "We create confusion, instill fear and capitalize on it at the same time. We already have militiamen in the state government, waiting for the appropriate time. For example, if the governor were to die suddenly, and the lieutenant governor were to become incapacitated, the state would have to resort to unusual means to restore the offices. That's where we come in with our men."

Stuart's mouth fell open.

"I'm talking about assassinating the governor and moving our people into power," Moreland said. "And you're the man that can make that possible. Your skill and training are exactly what we need to pull this off. And I promise you, I will make it worth your while."

Stuart took a swallow of the bourbon and forced himself not to shake his head in disbelief. He sat in shock as Moreland launched into a tirade about his militia, which Moreland lightly referred to as a "gun club."

Gun club my ass, Stuart thought. It's a terrorist organization!

Moreland began by explaining that the country, and the South in particular had gone straight to hell since the Sixties, since Vietnam, since that sonofabitch Johnson, since the Civil Rights Act, since the FBI had demolished the Mississippi Klan.

The liberals and their bastard ACLU lawyers—funded by the Jews—had stolen everything this country stood for and given it to the niggers, which had gotten us nowhere.

The country was decaying, Moreland said. Worse, it was regressing into an undisciplined, pathetic mob of Welfare babies sucking on the government tit.

"Just look around you," Moreland implored him. "Look what's happened to us. The entire nation is lazy, corrupt, and forevermore bowing down to minorities.

"The educational system has gone downhill every year since integration," Moreland said. "The number of Cadillacs and color TVs in front of the shanties in nigger town and the crime rate in the inner cities since blacks were given equality has gone up. Any fool could see where we're headed.

"And the media, those bastards, forced integration down the throats of good decent people in the South, while up in Boston schools were still segregated all the way to 1974!" Moreland continued. "And when the riots broke out and the National Guardsmen had to ride school buses in Boston, the media rationalized the whole thing away, claiming that at least it wasn't a bunch of racist rednecks like down south. Just like that bullshit with those civil rights workers that got what they deserved down in Philadelphia back in '64. The media, especially the movie makers, made those three out to be clean-cut Ivy League boys who were on a noble mission, when in fact they were a bunch of long-haired radicals down here with the sole purpose of stirring up the niggers so the newspapers would have a story."

Stuart gulped his drink and listened, both horrified and fascinated. Moreland sounded like the Baptist revival preachers he had seen on television as a boy.

"And that brought in the feds," Moreland said. "They terrorized the entire state into submission! The FBI destroyed the entire Ku Klux Klan in Mississippi. Almost."

Stuart shifted in his seat. He had grown up hearing the same argument that Moreland was now putting forth.

"About five years ago, Wade," Moreland said, "I noticed a grass-roots movement just getting started—a movement of white Americans. I watched the news and saw white people in places like Idaho, Oregon, and Illinois. Groups like the Michigan Militia and others were slowly waking up to the fact that the fate of the white race—not only in America, but the world—was not in the hands of the jackasses in Washington, but in theirs."

Moreland explained how he had listened to the news reports carefully. He had heard it all before, but this time was different. This wasn't a few KKK lynchings in 1964. This was organized. These groups communicated with one another, even trained one another. Secret enclaves nestled in the mountains and woods of America were the training grounds of the real future of White America.

"Then, it all became too clear to me, Wade," Moreland said. "I was no longer content to sit and watch. It was time to take a definite step in taking back what Americans deserved. It was time to wake this country up to the treason it was wallowing in and the corrupt government that's causing it. I had the basic structure, what was left of the Klan. I suddenly had the incentive to get the Klan back on its feet, but this time in the form of a militia. This time, there wouldn't be marches, cross burnings, anything obvious. No, this time it would be underground. Patience would be the real weapon of the militia."

Moreland stopped to take a breath. Stuart had recovered from his initial shock enough to start analyzing what Moreland was saying.

"But, Mr. Moreland," he said, "a militia needs weapons and training, and both of those are expensive, not to mention a good way to get you noticed by the feds."

Moreland smiled as if he were dealing with a slow child. "Sheriff Gage, Charlie, and I went to work, quietly recruiting, writing the mission of the militia, looking for prospective training sites, and collecting donations for weapons which would be needed when the time came," Moreland said. "We've been fairly successful."

Stuart knew from his briefings that the diligence of the three crusaders had paid off. Moreland had purchased a tract of woods in Junkin County—although it had cost him a fortune—as a base camp. There was no shortage of prospective trainees.

Moreland admitted that he was extremely proud of his recruiting. He had worked hard on his sales pitch, honed it to a polished finish. It worked.

Gage had set up the network to purchase and smuggle the guns into the state. Moreland didn't go into the details of this operation, as Stuart wished he had. Buying weapons in such a manner was more cumbersome than they realized, and that had slowed things down.

But the real problem, Moreland explained, was the lack of a training program for the trainees. Sure, Gage had been in Vietnam, but that was a long time ago, and besides he had a county which had laws to be upheld. And the trainees who had military training were in reality a bunch of cowboys who thought they knew a lot more about combat training than they actually did.

Enter Wade Stuart.

When Moreland saw a puzzled look on Stuart's face, he explained vaguely that Gage had "run a check" on him. With a little digging, Gage had been able to learn about Stuart's trips to the Middle East, including some work in Lebanon. The latter statement made Stuart more than a little uncomfortable.

"Wade, I'd planned on having this discussion with Tom present, but I didn't realize that you'd show up here with my niece," Moreland said. "But, anyway, what I'm asking you to do is design and implement a training program and to work directly and only with me on the other aspects."

Stuart took "the other aspects" to mean the assassination of the governor.

"It's got to be tough and realistic, no bullshit cowboy tough stuff," Moreland said. "I'm talking starting from basic marksmanship and moving up. I'm offering you a job as one of the key players in this organization." Moreland put both fists on his desk and leaned forward. His face turned ferocious. "But I am dead serious. And if you think about it, you'll know I'm right. I'm talking about all the things you were willing to risk your life for in defending this great country."

Yeah, you bastard, I'll train your people. And I'll rip your whole fucking operation apart. And gladly kill you if I have to, Stuart thought.

"Well, Mr. Moreland, it is quite a surprise. I didn't realize the scope of your operation," he said slowly, hoping his emotions were under control. "I'll just say it sounds intriguing. But you haven't mentioned exactly how much my time is worth"

Moreland said, "Fifty thousand dollars."

This time Stuart kept his mouth closed. He took the chance to get the initiative back from Moreland.

"A hundred thousand."

"Wade, fifty thousand dollars is a lot of money."

Stuart shrugged.

Moreland's mouth twitched slightly into a grin, as he said, "Seventy five thousand."

"Eighty."

"Son, I knew you were tough just by looking at you, but I didn't figure you to gouge me."

"Good help is hard to come by," Stuart said

"I take it this is your acceptance of the job?"

"For eighty thousand dollars, I'll surely think about it, Mr. Moreland."

"You've got two days." Moreland stood.

Stuart rose also and followed Moreland's gesturing hand to the door. As Stuart put his hand on the knob, he felt Moreland's heavy hand grasp his shoulder. He turned to see an extremely menacing Amos Moreland.

"Wade, you realize, if anything you heard today ever got out into the public, we'd have to make damn sure to take care of the leak, wherever it came from," Moreland said.

For the first time in many months, Wade Stuart felt the fear of the closeness of death.

"Believe me," he said, nodding. "I know all about the need for security."

"Wade!" Lee Ann shouted.

Stuart's head snapped up. Lee Ann was looking at him curiously.

"Are you deaf?" she asked.

"No...I...sorry. Didn't hear you."

"Obviously. Boy, you and Uncle Amos must've really hit it off," Lee Ann said.

"Where did you go?" Stuart said.

"Oh, I went to socialize while y'all got to know each other and do man talk," Lee Ann said, lowering her voice to say 'man talk.'

"Where'd the two of you go off to?"

"Oh, just inside for a talk. Let's go get something to eat," he said, pulling at her arm.

Still partly lost in thought, Stuart pulled her to the huge spread of food laid out on the long tables. He piled a paper plate high with barbecue ribs, potato salad, a baked potato, beans, and pecan pie. He and Lee Ann found a relatively quiet spot and sat on the lawn to eat.

After they finished their meal, they mingled, Lee Ann introducing Stuart to nearly everyone present. Stuart tried to concentrate on all the names, but his mind was still preoccupied. He made polite conversation and sipped beer, and wondered if the party would ever end.

At last, as the sun set, Lee Ann yawned. She led Stuart to the knot of people around Moreland, who seemed to be regaling the crowd with some tale or another. Occasionally, laughter would erupt, presumably, Stuart thought, at the appropriate time. They lingered at the edge of the small audience until Moreland broke free. Lee Ann said her good-byes and gave Moreland a hug. Moreland patted her back affectionately, then extended his hand to Stuart.

"Good to meet you, Wade. We'll talk more tomorrow."

"Yessir," Stuart said. "Good to meet you, too."

In the car, Lee Ann asked, "What was that all about—'we'll talk more tomorrow?'"

Stuart shrugged. "Your uncle wants to help me find a job."

"Really? That's great!"

"Yeah," Stuart said. "It's nice of him to do that."

"Oh, he's just that way."

Stuart looked at her for a long moment. She really doesn't know anything about her uncle Amos Moreland, he thought. He wondered if she'd think he was nice if he had him shot at sundown?

Early the next morning, Stuart hunched over his laptop computer, pounding the keyboard furiously as he reconstructed the previous day's meeting with Moreland. His head ached, the result of too much good food and strong bourbon—he had sat up for hours after returning from Lee Ann's apartment, staring through the window as he pondered the madness of Moreland's scheme. But he also wrestled with a dilemma. His mission had been to locate an alleged militia in Mississippi, identify the principals involved in a gun-smuggling operation and arrest them. He was certain he had done the first part of the mission, fairly confident he had done the second part, and had no idea how to go about accomplishing the third part.

Stuart knew that Moreland's ultimate goal was far more dangerous than a simple gun-smuggling operation, and he knew his bosses in Washington would see things that way as well. And Stuart knew that he was the only person who could stop Moreland from carrying out his plan. ATF, however, would demand an immediate arrest, but Stuart couldn't deliver. He needed more time to get inside the militia. Without evidence of that, he couldn't arrest anyone, let alone thwart Moreland.

All of Stuart's thoughts went into his e-mail message. After he finished, he re-read it, spell-checked it, then transmitted it.

He leaned back against the couch and rubbed his eyes, silently cursing himself for ever getting himself in this predicament.

Stuart's world was very black and white. He detested disorder. Everything had a place. At least that's what he used to think, he thought as we walked to the front window and peered at the thick stand of pine trees across the street. His mind struggled to place what was happening—and his values and beliefs—into the proper perspective. But he couldn't, and that angered him all the more.

Wade Stuart had committed his entire adult life to serving his country, and he considered himself to be the definition of a patriot. He'd worn his country's uniform and answered the call of battle on two separate occasions, risking his life each time. He was a federal agent, enforcing the laws of the nation to protect its citizens.

But—and Stuart shook his head disgustedly as he formed the thought—Moreland considered himself to be patriotic, too, which was insane. Or was it? Stuart hated to admit it, but he had found himself conceding at least a few points to Moreland in his tirade about the government becoming an ever-widening stain into American society.

But if that made Moreland right, what did it make him? A lackey? No, his way couldn't be the right one, but he wasn't making up some of his opinions about the federal government.

It had all seemed so simple years ago, on his commissioning day. Serve America. He'd done so the best way he knew how, in the Marines. He'd been naive, idealistic, a cherry boy, then. And like many young men with high ideals, he'd fought back the disillusionment that crept ever closer each time he saw an incompetent or unethical officer—and there had been plenty. Or given missions with only questionable legality, like the counternarcotics missions he'd apprehensively led in California's Mojave Desert.

As Stuart stared out the window, he slowly realized that the longer he served his country, the more he questioned its motives.

He'd been a good warrior, he told himself. He had fifteen ribbons in a shadowbox—two for bravery—to prove it.

And for what?

He'd come home from the Persian Gulf War to a military he'd hardly recognized, a Marine Corps obsessed with surviving budget cuts and a personnel drawdown. The Corps became a casualty of both, and the effect was the perverting of the service's ethos, *semper fidelis*, Latin for "always faithful." The post-Cold War attitude had been something akin to "Fuck you, I got mine," as officers barricaded themselves behind spotless records and searched for a benefactor to help them get promoted. As the careerism took hold, the "zero-defect" mentality inevitably followed. Any transgression, however small, was cause for a blemish on one's record, a kiss of death as far as promotion was concerned.

By the time Stuart had returned from the Persian Gulf, he knew the Desert Storm veterans were on the shitty end of the stick. Those who had remained in the States during the war had gotten the first whiff of the new wind and had already staked out their turf.

Stuart had watched in dismay as his combat-trained Marines— solid, hardworking Marines—were told they could not re-enlist because of the drawdown—their reward for serving their country bravely in war. He'd seen his friends in the officers' corps forced out of service by a low mark on a ten-year-old fitness report, or worse, relieved of their commands—a fatal blow to any officer's career—for no other reason than their battalion commander didn't like them.

Through it all, Stuart had stood his ground, only to have it washed from under his feet. He had trusted his friends, then felt the icy stab of their deceit as they betrayed him for their own careers. Stuart had always worn his integrity like a shiny coat of armor, and he'd watched it rust in the rain of time.

Finally, he had had enough. Like a prophet seeking justice but finding only distress, he walked from the ones who had sold their souls to a system he could no longer be a part of. He left the Marine Corps questioning many things, mostly himself. He looked for redemption, something to prove to him that he'd not been wrong to place his faith in a nation's system.

He'd found it in the ATF, a tightly knit group of professional agents committed to doing the right thing.

Or so he'd thought. An uncomfortable, familiar feeling swept over him. Stuart felt his value system being challenged, but this time like never before. He knew that if he redefined his values this time, then he would redefine himself.

Raymond Carr, Assistant Director of the Bureau of Alcohol, Tobacco and Firearms, sat at his desk in ATF headquarters in Washington, D.C. He sipped contentedly from his Brown University coffee cup, his second refill of the morning.

Carr, like many ATF agents, relished a routine, and his morning coffee was his. He usually spent the first forty-five minutes of his day easing into his workload over two or three cups made from beans he ground himself in a corner of his expansive, carpeted office. While enjoying his morning repose, he casually scanned the day's paperwork, prioritizing it according to importance and due dates.

Carr had just raised his cup to his lips when his computer chirped behind him, signaling the arrival of an electronic mail message. Carr frowned, thought about ignoring the artificial, sterile computer voice, then set his cup down. He didn't like e-mail this early in the morning.

He swiveled his chair, faced the computer, and grabbed the mouse to clear the aquarium-motif screen saver. He clicked the mouse on the icon for his e-mail program and peered at the screen.

The on-screen prompt informed him that the just-arrived message was "secure." Carr's interest was aroused, both at the classification and the hour at which it arrived. He clicked the mouse again to get to the password prompt, typed in his seven-character password, and watched the message blink onto the screen.

Stuart's message stunned him. Carr read it quickly, but intently. He was fascinated, horrified and satisfied by what he read. Fascinated because the plot was a great case, worthy of the total efforts of the ATF.

He was horrified by the scope and implications of the scheme, which represented his worst fear, indeed his own personal nightmare, of the militias across the United States.

Finally, he was satisfied that his agency had discovered the scheme. More accurately, he was satisfied that one of his most gifted special agents had discovered it. That was the reason Carr had approved of the operation by Stuart in the first place.

Carr finished reading and leaned back in his chair. As he let out a long breath, his mind raced. Stuart needed guidance, immediately.

The bureaucratic nature of the ATF, however, precluded Carr from responding at the moment. Carr smiled wryly at Stuart's last sentence—notice that he would contact Carr's office in twenty-four hours, as if confirming the bureaucracy's sluggish nature.

The assistant director was thankful for that. He'd have to brief the Director, and possibly the White House, before issuing Stuart further instructions.

He hunched before his screen for several minutes after reading Stuart's report. The assistant director tried to picture the young agent. He could almost feel the anxiety Stuart must surely be experiencing.

Carr, with over twenty-one years in ATF, was no stranger to

undercover work. He knew too well the treacherous path under-cover agents trod. His experience told him not to get overly emo-tional concerning Stuart's well-being, but the thought nagged at him.

He punched a button to print Stuart's report, then stood and removed the two-page document from the printer. As he left his office, turned right down a carpeted hallway, and walked to the director's office, he mentally prepared himself for the brief he was about to give. His only hope was that the process would be merciful enough to allow a quick response to Stuart.

5

S tuart yawned as he waited for Raymond Carr to answer the phone. It had been only three hours since he had returned from yet another weapons buy and transfer on the barrier island. He had managed a couple hours sleep before his mind told him to make a report to Washington, since he had heard nothing since his e-mail report five days earlier.

When Carr's secretary answered, Stuart identified himself and was immediately put on hold. He poured himself a cup of coffee from the machine on his kitchen counter, walked to the living room and sat in front of the small coffee table, on which sat a small notebook covered with small, neat handwriting.

"Good morning, Wade," Carr said when he finally answered.

Stuart returned the greeting and stared at his notes, preparing to report.

"Have you got anything more on Moreland's scheme to kill the governor?" Carr asked, which Stuart had expected.

"No, but let's talk about that later," Stuart said. "I want to give you the info on the smuggling."

"Okay, shoot," Carr said.

Stuart re-created the previous night's purchase in detail, which had been identical to the others. Stuart included a description of the skipper who had brought the weapons into the island. He included a time line, which would give Carr a good indication of how quickly the transaction had occurred, and, for good measure, he told Carr about his scuffle with Fat Man and Little Boy the week before.

Carr grunted and muttered, "Unbelievable."

"Yeah, that's what I thought at first," Stuart said as he sipped his coffee. "But, you know, it's working. I have to give them credit for that. And it's a pretty simple system. Buy the weapons up north. Finding a cowboy to bring them down the Intracoastal Waterway is easy these days. Retain one experienced skipper on contract in Florida, one with a powerful diesel boat. He picks the best date and time to make the run to the island.

"Unload before the smaller boats arrive for the distribution," Stuart continued. "The skipper receives the back half of his payment, sails away into the night, and never sees the other boats. In fact, he only sees two people the whole night, me and Tanner."

Stuart could picture Carr scribbling notes. "And it's always the same guy?" Carr said.

"Has been the four times I've been down there."

"How do the weapons get to the mainland?" Carr said.

"An hour or so later, five boats arrive, one by one, and in sequence," Stuart said. "The boat that gets the weapons has already been determined by Moreland, so Tanner and I just sit and wait until the right boat arrives. Tell the other four 'Thanks fellas, but not tonight, this will cover your fuel and time, see you next time.' Then we load the predetermined boat, send him on his way, then jump in our own boat and hightail it out of there. The weapons are met, somewhere between Waveland and Pass Christian, transferred to vehicles, and driven north for distribution."

"Sounds awfully simple," Carr said.

"It is," Stuart said. "So simple that a lot of weapons are coming into Mississippi undetected."

"Have you got enough evidence to make an arrest?"

Stuart smiled and shook his head at the anticipated question. "Not really," he said. "At this point, all I really know is that the MPM is smuggling weapons into Mississippi. I can link Gage, Tanner and Moreland to the operation, but there's still an awful lot I don't know, like how many weapons, where else they're being stored and who they're being distributed to. I still don't even know exactly who brings them or who Moreland is buying them from."

"Fair enough," Carr said. "But what about the assassination plot?"

Stuart detected the urgency in Carr's voice. "Moreland hasn't said anything else about it," Stuart said. "But that's another big unknown. I don't know the status of that scheme. I don't even know if Moreland really intends to go through with it and who's going to do it if he does."

Stuart had a thought. He spoke again. "Taking it one step further, what if he already has that plan in motion? If we take him down now, we may not stop the assassination—or find out who's doing the job."

Carr grunted at that. "Hadn't thought about it, but you're right," he said. "But you have to realize the urgency up here, Wade."

Stuart sighed and silently cursed the bureaucratic mentality that caused armchair warriors to try and call the shots from eight hundred miles away. "I understand," he said. "It's just not that easy. I'm walking a damn thin line out here. Moreland has already done some digging. He knows I'm a native. He knows I was in the Marine Corps—he even knows that I've got combat experience. This is a small state. It wouldn't be that difficult for him to do just a little too much digging and find out more about me than I care to think about."

Carr sighed. "Wade, I've been there, and believe me, I'm with you on this one," he said. "I even argued as much with the Director this morning. But the Director has his butt in the proverbial sling at the moment."

Carr told Stuart that the ATF director, Charles Norman, had prepared a brief for the President based on Stuart's earlier reports and had delivered an oral presentation in the Oval Office the previous day. It had not gone well.

"The director said he hadn't heard a President use such foul language in years," Carr said. "Norman said he was livid, especially since the President has made it his personal agenda to clamp down on terrorist organizations and militias in the country."

"Has the President ever heard of cause and effect?" Stuart said sarcastically. "Seems like you can't have one without the other. So I assume he's screaming for arrests?"

"Well, he's screaming, that's for damn sure," Carr said. "And that's reason enough for us to bring Moreland's operation to heel ASAP. But the director feels we have do it even faster than that."

Stuart was puzzled. He was working as fast as he could under the circumstances. "Why?"

Carr let out a deep breath and hesitated.

"Keep this quiet, Wade," he said. "Rumor has it that the President is using this as proof that the federal government has to take some definitive action, and he's going to use this as leverage to do something."

Stuart's anger flashed. He gripped the phone tightly. "He's going to get me killed!" he yelled into the phone. "As soon as he makes this public, Moreland's going to know I'm the leak."

"Calm down," Carr said. "He's not going public with it...yet. He's using the leverage here on the Hill."

"How?"

Carr muffled a chuckle. "Watch C-SPAN over the next few days. Congress ought to have some real interesting discussions about Posse Comitatus."

"You mean repealing it, don't you?" Stuart said.

Carr answered with silence.

"That's ridiculous," Stuart continued. "That won't solve anything. It might make matters worse."

Carr muttered a weak defense, but Stuart had already stopped listening. He grabbed the television remote control and turned the channel to C-SPAN. In a deserted House chamber, a representative stood at a podium and droned on about nothing in particular, but proving to his constituents that they were getting their money's worth with him in office.

"That's why you have to shut these guys down as fast as you can," Carr said.

"Okay, but it won't be easy," Stuart said, then broke the connection.

Stuart threw the phone onto the couch and stared at the television. Repealing Posse Comitatus? What will those idiots think of next?

It wasn't much of a compound, not to anyone even moderately trained in the intricacies of the military. It was actually a collection of buildings that resembled squatter's shacks more than anything else.

Four of these structures formed the core of the compound in a clearing hacked out of a dense pine forest. The buildings were aligned in roughly a square, and the well-worn dirt around them fell away gently in all directions.

Stuart viewed the scene from the passenger side of a pickup truck driven by Gage. When Gage stopped, Stuart got out and walked past the main compound area in the cool dark shadows of evening twilight.

He walked to the southern edge of the clearing, past a row of evenly spaced small wooden boxes. On the ground surrounding each of the boxes was a considerable amount of brass—expended cartridges—from a variety of weapons. After speaking with Carr, Stuart had spent the week constructing the rifle range with the help of some of Moreland's militiamen.

The firing line faced a long, relatively flat corridor, also carved out of the forest with chainsaws, which extended about five hundred yards into the woods. Tall, thick trees bordered the range on three sides and acted to muffle the reports of the automatic weapons, shotguns, and pistols fired by shooters on the ready boxes on the firing line.

At the forest end of the range, a low dirt berm rose and fell unevenly across the width of the range. Behind it, crude metal frames stood spaced apart to match the boxes on the other end. These frames would hold paper or wooden targets—a silhouette of a man from the groin up—when the firing line was "hot."

Stuart and Gage strolled past the targets, the sheriff quietly watching as Stuart professionally inspected the range. They stepped behind the target line into the "butts," as the dozen or so people who had fired there recently had learned to call it. The butts consisted simply of piles of dirt along the width of the range which acted as an impact area for the projectiles, to prevent rounds from sailing deeper into the forest and possibly hitting an unwary person.

Stuart gazed back at the compound from the range. He was just as disgusted with the shoddy little dump today as he had been a week ago.

He wasn't sure what he had really expected to see then, when he finally met some of the militiamen and watched them train, but what he had seen so far did nothing to impress him as to the fighting ability of Moreland's rednecks.

The decrepit dirt track that served as an access road allowed only one way in and out of the place, except by foot. The road was manned at what could only be an arbitrary point—it certainly held no military value—by two slouching, surly good ol' boys with shotguns slung carelessly over their shoulders.

The guards controlled further access to the road by opening and closing a steel cattle gate after identifying the driver. Stuart had looked in vain for an outpost, another guard in the woods to the side of the road to reinforce the gate guards.

He had not even seen a strand of barbed wire, or any form of communications between the guards and the compound they were supposedly protecting.

Stuart thought about this as he walked back to the main compound, which was in no better shape. About twenty men and, to Stuart's surprise, a few women lolled about, the men shuffling aimlessly with their hands in their pockets, the women chatting near the buildings. No guards were in sight, no towers for observation, and, again, no protective wire around the site. Stuart's thorough military mind had taken all this information and processed it on two levels.

The first level was as a military mission in which he would have to make some immediate and drastic improvements. This was necessary to give him some credibility with Moreland and seem serious about his role here.

The second was analytical, as if he were an infiltrator, which he was, taking in the weaknesses of the compound and the people within, measuring, memorizing, and planning an efficient, violent method of destroying the place.

As Stuart looked across the compound, he was aware that he was holding two contradictory thoughts in his mind at once. He had to improve the place, but not to the point where he would be unable to take it down. Of course, he reasoned, only he would know which weaknesses still remained.

But, even with all the work he had done, Stuart had still spent most of the last week worrying. His call to the assistant director had been followed by more e-mail reports on Moreland's gun-smuggling operation and information on Moreland, Gage and Tanner. All had so far produced disappointing results. He knew better than to expect quick results from the pogues in D.C.

"Hey, Wade, you with the livin'?" Gage said as he walked up, startling Stuart.

Stuart nodded. "Yeah, I was just thinking about all the training we still have to do."

"Well, come on, I'll show you something that ought to make it easier," Gage said as he walked toward one of the compound buildings.

Stuart complied, and followed Gage. The sheriff walked toward one of the "barracks" that was being used as a warehouse.

"I saw you firing on the range the other day," Gage said as they walked. "I have to tell you I was impressed. Ain't every day somebody can put eight out of ten rounds into an eight-inch

group on a man-sized target from five hundred yards away."
Stuart shrugged. "Just the result of good training," he said.
Gage nodded. "That kind of training can do us a lot of good."
The sheriff unlocked the door to the warehouse and swung it
open, slapping the light switch as he did so. He stepped aside as
Stuart entered the building.

Stuart, although his face didn't show it, was aghast. At least a
hundred—there could have been more—boxes of M16A2 service
rifles stood in one corner. Boxes of grenades, ammo and flares
were also stacked against the wall. Stuart looked at Gage, who
grinned.

"Tanner picked up a big shipment last week while you were out
here," Gage said. "This gives us just about all the firepower we
can handle."

"How in the hell can we afford it?" Stuart asked, amazed.

"You'd be surprised, Wade," Gage said in a way that suggest-
ed he would not entertain further questions about the acquisition.

"Shit," Stuart said, mentally inventorying the weaponry for a
future report to Washington.

"We can really start training now, the way you planned," Gage
said as he gestured for Stuart to exit the building. "Most of this
ammo is blanks, so we can do it realistically."

Stuart stepped outside the warehouse. Gage slammed and
locked the door and the two walked toward the truck.

"Yeah, that's great," Stuart said, hoping he sounded enthusias-
tic. "I'll start working on it next week."

Gage smiled. "Yeah, I figured you'd want to get right on it," he
said. "Look, I have to get back to work, but I'll give you a lift
back into town."

"That's fine," Stuart said.

Stuart leaned back against the wall of Moreland's study and
watched his reaction. Moreland sat on the other side of the room
on an overstuffed couch. Tanner sat on a chair next to them.
They had just heard Stuart's plan for finishing the construction

of the MPM compound—the range had only been Phase One, Stuart had explained—and the training of the militiamen. Stuart had even taken the time to prepare visual aids, which rested on an easel to his right.

Stuart's plans impressed Moreland immensely. Tanner barely reacted, which came as no surprise to Stuart, who reasoned that Tanner resented him for taking over a project he had thought of as his own. Stuart said nothing, but continued to mentally file information about the man he viewed as potentially his most dangerous adversary, especially after the incident with Fat Man and Little Boy.

After the meeting broke up, Stuart drove to his apartment. He quickly prepared a meal and devoured it, then put the dishes away as therapy for his preoccupied mind. Stuart hated waiting, whether in a ticket line or for an expected package in the mail. He was now forced to wait out Moreland, the militia, the ATF. It gnawed at him, turning him impatient and short-tempered. Snatching a beer from the refrigerator he decided against calling Lee Ann. Instead, he flopped down on the couch and glared at the ceiling for a long time. He thought back on the times when he felt hopeless because of a few deskbound government wonks who couldn't make a decision.

He recalled the night when he was in the second grade, living with his parents in Meridian. It was 1968, the year that tore the country apart. With Vietnam, "long, hot summers" and integration ripping the fabric of America, no one was completely sane.

It was also the time when the FBI finally arrested its suspects in the murder of three civil-rights workers in Philadelphia, Mississippi, after four years of investigation. Those years had gnawed at the people of Mississippi, and the arrests, which included the county sheriff, brought emotions to a boil.

In Meridian, the site for the trial, the Ku Klux Klan began flexing its considerable muscle. The KKK wasn't about to back down from the feds, even though it was well-publicized that the FBI's arrests were made possible only by infiltrating the Klan with its agents. The Klan openly flaunted its presence and supposed power, and even began an aggressive recruiting campaign to capitalize on the emotions of white Mississippi.

Stuart's father had been a target of this recruitment effort. Frank Stuart, however, was fiercely independent and had no time—nor respect—for the KKK. Descended from three generations of sharecroppers, Frank Stuart had lived side-by-side with blacks his entire life, and all the white sheets in the world weren't going to change his attitude.

When Frank told a Klansman to "go piss up a rope," the KKK immediately put him under surveillance, partly to pressure him and partly to see if he would report the Klan contact to the feds. Frank did neither. Never a man to back down, he knew he was being watched. He waited for an opportune moment, and found one on a winter day in downtown Meridian.

His driver's license required renewal, so Frank drove to the highway patrol office in the federal building. As he ascended the steps, he noticed a water fountain. Actually, there were two—one marked "Whites Only" and the other "Colored." Knowing a Klansman watched from a few feet, Frank went directly to the "colored" fountain and took a long drink.

The Klan exhibited its wrath just two nights later. While Frank worked the night shift, his family went to bed. At 2:30 a.m., Mrs. Stuart received a phone call. A male voice asked her if she had been paying attention to the recent rash of bombings in the area, aimed at black churches and Jewish synagogues. When Mrs. Stuart sleepily replied that she had, the voice said, "You're next," and hung up.

Terrified for her son and his younger sister, Annabelle Stuart immediately called the police. An officer responded in less than ten minutes and carried the children to safety at a neighbor's house across the street.

A search by a bomb disposal team discovered nothing, Wade learned years later.

But, he could still vividly remember waking up in the arms of a police officer, his forehead scraping against the officer's badge on a cold, jet-black night.

Years later, Stuart would place part of the blame for that night on an FBI that moved at the pace of a glacier.

Not this time, Stuart thought as he stared at the ceiling.

6

The U. S. Senator from Georgia, Lyman Ellis, was midway through his speech before a joint session of the United States Congress. Stuart watched the scene on the C-SPAN channel in his apartment while Lee Ann slept in his bed.

"Ladies and gentlemen, I must defer to my distinguished colleague from the grand state of Virginia on his passionate and most appropriate remarks regarding the future of this great nation," Ellis said.

At the enraged insistence of the President—after the ATF's report on the Mississippi People's Militia—a resolution calling for the repeal of the Posse Comitatus law was before the legislative body, and both sides were making their pitches.

Due mainly to the fervent pleas of the congressmen from Virginia and Mississippi, and now Ellis' eloquent demand for action, the doves were losing ground.

"Let us remember that our own homes, the homes of our proud, freedom-loving ancestors are at stake," Ellis said. "We are not talking about a conflict far from our shores, a conflict that we can observe with a distant eye. We are speaking of Americans who may be soon fighting for their very lives right in their own homes, within our borders. How can we rightfully call ourselves the leader of the free world if we refuse to defend our own citizens when they so desperately need us?" Ellis paused as applause thundered from his supporters.

Ellis continued to enthrall his audience for another twenty minutes. Probably the most skilled orator in Congress, he swayed many opinions this morning. He had to. He was the last speaker, and the vote on the resolution would be taken immediately after his speech.

When he finished speaking, he received a standing ovation, even from some of his most steadfast opponents.

The Speaker of the House called the long list of names to record the votes of the senators and representatives gathered for the momentous occasion. No one was absent. Each knew the exact number of votes needed to pass or defeat the resolution. When the vote passing the resolution was cast, the chamber erupted in cheering and applause that certainly did not fit the dignity of the United States Congress. Twice the Speaker had to call for order as the rest of the votes were tallied.

When the last name had been called, Senator Ellis sighed, grinning broadly as he slumped back in his leather chair. Dozens of supporters were shaking his hand, congratulating him, and slapping him on the shoulder. He thanked them sincerely for their support on the resolution.

The Speaker of the House called for order once more, and the din in the House Chamber settled to a hum. The Speaker cleared his throat, and announced, "By a vote of four hundred and twenty three 'ayes' to one hundred and twelve 'nays,' the resolution is passed. This session is adjourned."

Stuart watched, stupefied. Lee Ann awoke and slipped onto the couch beside him, wearing only a T-shirt that was much too short.

Are they crazy? he thought. He couldn't believe what he was hearing and what it meant. Congress was opening the door for the use of federal troops—Stuart would bet the Marine Corps—to do what essentially amounted to the ATF's job—law enforcement. Preventing the use of the military in this manner was, of course, exactly the purpose of the Posse Comitatus Law.

And, more importantly, Stuart thought, this was exactly what these militias have been ranting about for years. They predicted that this day would come, and Congress was making their warnings—their dreams—come true. It was preposterous, it was dangerous, and it played right into the hands of militias across the country.

This isn't a rebellion, there is no armed enemy, Stuart thought, although he knew that those words would get some air play very soon, if his hunch was correct.

He reasoned that Congress or the President, or both, intended to paint a picture of an open rebellion in Mississippi, then send in troops to crush it in an effort to set an example, to punish those responsible for recent bombings and to send a clear message to those who may be contemplating more.

Stuart shook his head in disgust. This was exactly what Moreland, and countless others like him, wanted: the evil federal government showing its true colors.

Lee Ann continued to watch carefully. She asked a few thoughtful questions, which Stuart answered absently.

Moreland must be dancing with joy, Stuart thought. And he'd want a meeting. He rose to the couch and walked to the phone. No sense in waiting for him to call.

Moreland gestured wildly as he ranted about the Evil Government, which was proving his predictions, proving to the American people that America was dead and freedom vanquished.

"Those bastards in Washington will stop at nothing to take away the freedom of the people," Moreland fumed. "They're traitors, outlaws, and thieves, the sonsofbitches!"

Stuart stood patiently, waiting for Moreland to cool off.

Again, Stuart found himself agreeing with at least part of what Moreland was saying. He, too, questioned the prudence—if not the legality, as Moreland did—of the congressional resolution to repeal Posse Comitatus.

Stuart was familiar with the provisions of the law, and very familiar with the razor-thin line between the military being used for national security purposes and participation in law-enforcement activities.

That line was so thin it was nearly invisible. For some years, the military had been assisting local law-enforcement agencies dealing with drug smugglers. Stuart himself had participated in several of these missions, all of which didn't exist officially. The missions skirted the Posse Comitatus law by couching them in bureaucratic mumbo-jumbo and labeling them as matters of national security.

The missions, as explained to Stuart by two very important Army lieutenant colonels, were also legal because the law, while prohibiting the use of the military in the actual apprehension of suspected criminals, did not forbid the military from providing "surveillance assistance," as in the case of Stuart's unit, an infantry company in the 1st Marine Division.

Stuart never fully resolved in his own mind the legality of those missions, and now, in Moreland's office, the old doubt seeped back into his mind. He struggled with the answer until Moreland exhausted himself and collapsed heavily into his chair.

He looked up at Stuart. "You know what their next step is, don't you?" Moreland asked.

"Sure as hell sounds like they're considering sending in troops."

"Exactly." Moreland banged his fist on the steel desk. He stared at Stuart. "Tell me, Wade, you used to be in the Marine Corps, what do you make of this?"

Stuart sighed and shifted his weight. He felt as if Moreland was reading his mind.

"When I joined the Marines, I took an oath to defend the Constitution of the United States against all enemies, foreign and domestic," he said. "That meant a lot to me. It seemed pretty clear at the time. But after the Cold War ended and it looked like the military would have to justify its budget just to stay alive, we started getting missions that really made me think about the part in the oath about 'all enemies foreign and domestic,' especially when we started doing counternarcotics missions."

Moreland leaned back in his chair. Stuart saw that he was intrigued and pressed on. It felt good to talk about a part of his military career that had bothered him for years.

"I remember squatting behind a rock in a national park out in the Mojave Desert in California, tracking smugglers as they brought their dope through the desert," Stuart said. "I just sat there and watched them with night-vision goggles. They were armed, but not like my Marines. We were up in the hills, and all the smugglers had a weapon aimed at their heads. None of my guys would have hesitated a second to waste a dope dealer. And that bothered me."

"Why?" Moreland asked.

"One itchy trigger finger, one loose rock rolling down a hillside, and I would've had a full-blown firefight on my hands," Stuart said. "The political ramifications of that were just unbelievable. And that's when I started to doubt the legality of what the government is doing. If politics played into that so much, then why the hell were we doing it? I'm not sure that dope smugglers are a 'domestic enemy' to the Constitution."

Moreland pounded the desk again. The noise was deafening in the small room. "Exactly. And this is another example. The federal government is doing whatever it can to take over every aspect of this nation. We don't have a lot of time—and we have to start thinking about defending ourselves."

"That's why I'm here," Stuart said, glad to change the subject. "I'm going to Biloxi tonight to pick up a shipment of weapons."

"Good. Don't waste any time down there. We need those weapons up here as fast as you can get them," Moreland said.

7

The Hinds County Courthouse was an imposing structure of gray concrete. Its huge facade loomed darkly in downtown Jackson, Mississippi, the state capital.

The building sat among the Jackson Police Department building; the offices of Jackson's leading daily newspaper, the *Clarion-Ledger*; and City Hall. To the front, State Street carried government workers and tourists past the courthouse's needlelike cement sculpture that squatted in front of the building that was vaguely reminiscent of something out of a George Orwell novel.

On this Monday morning, however, it was scarcely noticed by the hundreds of people who scurried to their offices. Government employees, businessmen, and secretaries charged down the street, shoulders hunched and heads down in the peculiar manner of modern urban dwellers.

The dozens of people who ascended or descended the concrete steps of the Hinds County Courthouse were oblivious to rush-hour traffic, much less one small blue delivery truck bearing the logo "Williams' Freight Delivery" on its side.

The truck slowed to the curb in front of the building and stopped. The driver, dressed in blue coveralls with a white name patch over the left breast pocket which read "Steven" climbed out of the truck. He jammed a company baseball cap on his head and checked the clipboard in his left hand.

The driver strolled to the back of the truck and raised the sliding door. He climbed inside, checked the number on a box against the number on his clipboard and jumped casually from the back of the truck, pulling the door down as he did so. He then checked his watch again and walked up the steps into the courthouse.

Inside, he turned right, down a dimly lighted corridor, checking the numbers on the doors. About halfway down the long corridor he saw an exit sign.

Apparently not finding the office he sought, he went through the exit and down a flight of stairs to a door which led to the outside of the building. He pushed the door open and stepped onto a sidewalk across from the police department.

The driver looked both ways, then quickly unzipped his coveralls and stepped out of them.

Underneath, he wore light gray cotton trousers, a white button-down shirt and a patterned burgundy tie. He rolled his cap and clipboard up in the coveralls, then turned right and walked to the street in front of the courthouse. As he passed a dumpster in the alley, he deposited the coveralls.

When he reached the sidewalk adjacent to the street where his truck was parked, he turned left—away from the truck—and walked down the street, an anonymous government employee going to work on a Monday morning.

Inside the truck sat six fifty-five-gallon drums filled with homemade napalm, an incendiary substance used extensively by the U.S. military since the later days of World War II. Unlike military-grade manufactured napalm, however, this had been made by mixing large quantities of gasoline and powdered laundry detergent. This concoction, which turned jelly-like when mixed, was known in military circles as "fugas" and had the same explosive effects as manufactured napalm.

During the Vietnam War, fugas was used mainly as a defensive weapon. Placed on a slope, a drum of fugas could be "command-detonated" by placing a Claymore mine or a blasting cap and a small charge of plastic explosive on the back side of the drum. Basically an electrical circuit, the charge or the mine could be detonated by completing the circuit. The exploding charge ignited the fugas and blew the flaming jelly at the enemy, invariably cutting a hideous swath in its path.

The two men staring at the truck from a building across the street knew this—it was they who had built the bomb. They planned to detonate it differently, however. Rather than use an electrical circuit, these trigger men would detonate the initial charge by radio-wave transmitter. A receiver attached to a small block of plastic explosive, which was in turn attached to one of the drums, would receive the signal and detonate the blasting cap, thus triggering the explosive train.

Neither man knew how much explosive power the bomb would produce, but this wasn't important to them. What was important was simply that the bomb would explode; the explosion itself would be enough to accomplish their mission.

From their second-story vantage point, the men had an unobstructed view of the front of the courthouse and the street fifty yards in either direction. One of the men held a pair of two-hundred-power binoculars to his eyes and focused on the deadly blue truck parked below. To his left, his partner leaned on the windowsill with both elbows. At his feet sat a small radio transmitter.

"Looks good," said the man with the binoculars. "How long's it been since he got out of the truck?"

"Almost six minutes," replied the second man as he pushed himself from the sill, stooped and picked up the transmitter. "Two more minutes."

"Right." The man with the binoculars didn't avert his gaze from the truck.

The mission had been planned and rehearsed. Eight minutes after the driver left the parked truck, the men in the window would detonate the bomb. The two trigger men were at a relatively safe distance across the street, as the bomb was directional. It had been constructed so that most of the explosive force would be delivered toward the front of the courthouse.

"Get ready," the man with the transmitter said, staring intently at his watch.

The man with the binoculars moved to the right of the window and stood with his back against the wall. "Ready," he said.

The man with the transmitter mirrored his partner's movements, to the left of the window. He held the transmitter in his right hand. Without taking his eyes off his watch, he pressed a button on the transmitter with the second hand of his watch swept up to the eight-minute mark.

A terrific sound of rushing air, instantly followed by a deafening explosion, ripped through the still early-morning air. Although aimed away from them, the men in the office felt the heat of four hundred and forty pounds of napalm igniting and felt the concussion slam against them through the wall. Their decision to stand clear of the window saved their lives, as the shock wave shattered the window and flung shards of glass into the opposite wall.

On the street below, seventeen people died outright, burned horribly by the fireball that raced up the steps and into the building and set it on fire. The concussion destroyed four of the building's external columns, causing the roof to collapse and pinning three people under tons of concrete rubble.

Inside, in the main lobby, dozens of people were blown off their feet. Several were burned, either by the burning jelly sailing through the lobby or by secondary fires ignited by the napalm. The explosion splintered nearly every piece of wood on the first floor, shattered glass, and launched furniture, glass and metal through the air.

Those not initially injured staggered to their feet and stumbled aimlessly through the wreckage. On the floors above, employees felt the floor shudder beneath them and heard the explosion. Many, sensing danger, raced down the stairs and into an inferno.

Fire completely consumed the first floor. Several mangled or burned corpses littered the floor amidst the rubble. Fire raged in the old structure, out of control and oblivious to the horrified screams of the injured and dying.

Several employees braved the flames and dense, choking smoke in an attempt to rescue the injured. Some, viewing the carnage, sank to their knees and vomited. Still others became trapped or injured themselves trying to escape.

Within three minutes, the fire was completely out of control, threatening the lives of over a hundred employees, including three justices of the Mississippi Supreme Court.

Pandemonium reigned inside and out on the street. In a macabre signature of the bomb, the sidewalk and steps leading to the entrance of the building were blackened, charred by the intense heat of the blast.

Traffic immediately choked the street as panicked drivers jammed on their brakes and caused several accidents, one serious. These pile-ups blocked the street completely, which would soon hamper rescue efforts.

Across the street, shaken and dazed office workers peered out through destroyed window panes. Most were only slowly comprehending what had just happened. Some began to filter out onto the street, but most simply stared out the window in shock.

The two trigger men carefully made their way out of their office and down the stairs. They assumed looks of disbelief as they exited the building. For a few minutes, they surveyed the damage with the growing crowd. Then they quietly broke away from the throng and moved down the street, completely unnoticed.

Stuart reflexively dove deeper under the bed covers, curling up as he did so, determined to ignore the ringing of the phone, but when it did not stop, he flung the sheets to the floor and leaped across the room toward the cordless phone.

"Did you see it? Can you believe it?" Lee Ann asked.

"What are you talking about?" Stuart asked.

"Haven't you seen the news this morning?"

"No." He glanced around the bedroom for a T-shirt.

"Well, turn it on," Lee Ann said.

"Okay, okay," Stuart said, pulling a shirt over his head. He walked to his television set and turned it on. "What channel?"

"Any channel, it doesn't matter."

Stuart watched the picture form on his screen. He saw the front of what looked like a government building—or what had been a government building. The structure now resembled those Stuart had seen in Kuwait City in 1991, except this one was still aflame. His reaction of curiosity changed to one of confusion, then realization, then anger. He listened intently as the reporter spoke over the images of destruction.

"...there are no suspects and no motive as of yet, or even a determination as to whether this is an act of terrorism or a tragic accident," said the reporter, a brunette from Channel 7. "Initial reports are that at least fifty people are dead, hundreds injured and an undetermined number still trapped inside the burning building. It would appear..."

Stuart snatched the remote control from the couch and muted the volume. He felt a stab of ice in the pit of his stomach. This was no accident.

"Lee Ann," he asked, "when did this happen?"

"Early this morning, around eight o'clock," she replied. "Who would do something like this, Wade? Just kill all those people for no reason?"

Stuart had an idea who, and he was sure he knew their reason.

"I don't know," he said absently. He tried to recount everything he'd heard or seen with the Mississippi People's Militia the last few weeks. "Has anybody taken responsibility for the bombing?"

"No," Lee Ann answered, puzzled. "Why?"

"Standard terrorist tactics," he explained. "If this is a terrorist attack, and it sure looks like one, a group always claims responsibility."

"Do you think this is another terrorist attack?" she asked.

"Yeah, I do," Stuart said, growing impatient. He had to act immediately. "The whole point is to gain attention. What you're watching is exactly what they want—attention. Look, I have to get going. Can I call you back later?"

"Yeah, sure," Lee Ann said sadly. "Wade?"

"Yeah?"

"Is anyone safe anymore?"

Stuart stared at the wall. "I don't think any place has ever been very safe, Lee Ann. We're just now learning that." He hung up the phone and frantically dressed.

Already, he was cursing Moreland and his militia. He also cursed Moreland because, even if the MPM wasn't responsible for what he was watching, Stuart's life had just become exponentially more difficult. The ATF would be screaming for answers and Stuart had none. His distraction had been complete and perfect. He had to get to Moreland immediately, before getting on the horn with the ATF.

He sat on the couch and watched the continuing coverage of the bombing.

The reporter pulled an eyewitness into the frame beside her and asked for his description of what had happened. The view cut to an overhead shot from the helicopter normally used for traffic reports as the eyewitness, a male civil servant, described the blast.

"I heard this explosion," he said. "I was facing away from the building when it went and the concussion slammed me against the wall. There was all kinds of glass flying around and then the fire started. I ran inside, in the main lobby, and saw a whole bunch of people on the floor. Some were burned, either by what looked like napalm—I'm a Vietnam vet—or by other fires. There was wood and glass everywhere and furniture had been blown all over the place."

The reporter cut in again to tell viewers that the witness had rescued four people and had burned his hands badly in the process. The man held his hands up to the camera. Stuart frowned, grabbed a notebook from the dining room table and began taking notes.

Other witnesses—survivors—told horrifying tales of employees on the upper floors of the building falling to the first floor when ceilings gave way. Several victims described fires that consumed the first floor and how they had to step over mangled or burned corpses littered across the floor amidst the rubble. Stuart angrily turned the television off and left the apartment.

The car slid sideways in the loose gravel of the MPM main compound as Stuart jammed on the brakes. The drive from his apartment had worked him into a full-blown rage and he was about to vent it on Moreland.

Stuart stomped across the open ground to the headquarters building which housed Moreland's office. He scarcely noticed that no one was in the area. He flung open the door to Moreland's office with such force the door smacked heavily against the wall.

Amos Moreland sat behind his desk. He barely flinched. He merely lifted his eyes to Stuart, a hint of a smile drifting across his face.

Stuart, his face dark, interpreted Moreland's expression as confirmation of his suspicions.

"You sonofabitch," Stuart said. "You did it, didn't you? You blew up that courthouse."

Moreland shifted in his seat, sighed and gestured for Stuart to sit. Stuart remained standing, hands loosely at his side. Moreland shrugged.

"Yes," Moreland said. "We set that up a long time ago."

"You sneaky bastard," Stuart said. "Why wasn't I informed of this? What the hell kind of games are you playing, Moreland?"

"Games? If you think this is a game, then you're not as smart as I thought you were," Moreland said. "And you of all people should know about compartmented information and the need to know."

"You blow up the Hinds County Courthouse and I don't have a need to know? I'm not some redneck lackey and you know it," Stuart said. "I should have been part of this from the start."

"Maybe," Moreland said. "But you weren't. And that's the end of it. Besides, it's over and done with and it went fairly well."

"Who was the trigger man?" Stuart asked.

"Men, actually," Moreland replied. "Two men who specialize in this kind of work. I don't know who they are. Never met 'em. Never plan to."

Stuart forced himself to calm down. "Well, they sure did a hell of a job," he said with a forced smile he hoped looked natural.

Moreland chuckled. "Yes, they did."

"Who was in charge of the operation? Gage?"

"Charlie did all the contacting—and coordinating," Moreland said. "I selected the target."

Stuart had already guessed that Tanner coordinated the attack. He swore at himself for not taping this conversation.

"Great target," Stuart said. "If the intent was to commit a terrorist act for max shock—and media attention."

"Exactly our intent," Moreland said. He smirked. "Marines aren't the only ones who study terrorism."

"You're right," Stuart said. He'd searched for students of terrorism for years. "But why the courthouse? Why not the Governor's Mansion?"

"This morning three justices from the state Supreme Court were in that building. We had a chance to cripple the state's highest court," Moreland said with a trace of satisfaction.

"How did you and Tanner pull it off?"

Moreland rose and opened a wall locker in one corner of his office. He produced a cardboard tube about four feet long. Back at his desk, he pulled several rolled-up papers, each about three feet square and spread them out on his desk. He beckoned for Stuart to look closer.

Stuart saw that the top sheet was a scale map, and—from the aerial television shots he had seen less than an hour earlier—he recognized it as a map of the Hinds County Courthouse and the immediate vicinity.

Moreland, taking his time, explained the bombing in detail, in chronological order in a way that told Stuart that the operation had most likely been rehearsed many times before its execution.

Stuart nodded. He was impressed. "What kind of explosives did you use? What I saw on TV didn't look like fertilizer residue."

"That's because it wasn't," Moreland said. "After Oklahoma City, nobody can get that stuff in the quantities you need. This was napalm."

"How did you get that?" Stuart said, then answered his own question. "You made it yourself, didn't you?"

Moreland nodded. "A lot of gasoline and powdered laundry detergent, mixed and poured into a half-dozen fifty-five-gallon drums and put inside the truck."

"What the Marine Corps calls fugas," Stuart said.

"Yep," Moreland said. "And it's just as good as the manufactured stuff."

Stuart nodded. He had constructed similar bombs. He was familiar with the effects of a well-placed barrel of napalm.

"So now what? What did it really accomplish, except pissing off the feds and scaring the shit out of the whole state?" Stuart said.

"You're looking at it wrong," Moreland said. "This wasn't the climax, it was the first step. Act One. This was just to get folks' attention. We've got a few other surprises before we take down the governor."

"Such as?"

"Need to know," Moreland said, shaking his head.

"Let's not go through that again," Stuart said. "That's bullshit and you know it. If you're not going to trust me, this isn't going to work."

"Oh, it'll work just fine," Moreland said coldly. His eyes locked with Stuart's. "After all, what are you going to do—quit? Do you think I'm going to let you just walk out of here now?"

Stuart realized that he was a dead man as soon as he was no longer necessary. He took a deep breath and exhaled loudly.

"Okay, Amos," he said.

Moreland smiled. "Good. Now, like I said, this is only the beginning. We have to pick up the pace, get things moving. I need you to go down to Electric Mills to distribute some weapons to another group. Charlie's busy this week setting up another purchase, so you're on your own."

Stuart shook his head. "Okay, but I need a couple of days," he said. "I'm getting behind at school and I've got a class tomorrow."

Moreland frowned.

Stuart shrugged helplessly.

"All right," Moreland said. "You can go to class tomorrow. But can you make the run tomorrow night?"

Stuart nodded. "Shouldn't be a problem," he said.

In Washington, Raymond Carr's daily routine had been shattered. Within minutes of the explosion in Mississippi, approximately 11:30 a.m. Eastern Time, Carr's phone and computer lit up, blinking and chiming, respectively.

Unaccustomed to a sudden influx of activity, Carr was momentarily overwhelmed. Like Stuart, Carr ran the gamut of confusion, realization and rage. Unlike Stuart, however, Carr was hardly able to put any of the information flooding into his office into any coherent form. He simply didn't have a feel for what had happened and in what order.

After the first barrage of phone calls, one from the director, Carr jabbed at his remote control, bringing CNN to his television screen. As the images of carnage came from the corner of his office, Carr temporarily forgot about the phone and the computer. He watched, coldly furious, as grim-faced firefighters pulled people—some alive, but many dead—from the dense black smoke and blasted rubble of the courthouse. Revulsion consumed him as he watched, transfixed.

When he wrenched his eyes from the horror, Carr snapped back into reality. He answered the calls rapidly, tersely barking out the same reply to the same question—no, he didn't know, reports were still coming in.

Which he hoped was true, as he turned his attention to his computer screen. Already, he had eleven e-mail messages. Scanning each, he fired off the same response: "No info—will contact you later." He knew that Stuart would be checking in, but none of the messages were from him.

"Shit!" Why hadn't Stuart warned them? And why hadn't he reported in yet?

The door to his office flew open. The doorway was filled with the hulking, glaring frame of the Director of the Bureau of Alcohol, Tobacco and Firearms, Charles Norman.

"Goddamnit, Ray, I thought you had a man down there precisely for this sort of thing!" Norman snapped as Carr spun away from his computer screen and jumped to his feet.

"I do, Charles, I do," Carr said, somewhat defensively.

"Well, what the hell happened?" Norman entered Carr's office and closed the door—without slamming it.

"I don't know. He should have let us know, warned us. It doesn't make sense. I'm still waiting to hear from him." Carr paused as if he'd just realized something. "Charles, for all I know, he's dead."

The director's eyebrows shot up. From the sick look on Carr's face, Norman could tell his deputy was serious.

"When was the last time—"

"About three days ago," Carr replied, anticipating the question. "A lot can happen in three days."

"I think we've just seen evidence of that," Norman said, his tone softer. "Ray, find out if he's still alive. Do whatever you have to do to contact him. I just came from the White House."

Carr cast a quizzical look at his boss.

"The plot on the governor," Norman said. "I was almost done with the brief when the CNN report came on. The president went nuts. He was absolutely outraged. I will not repeat his exact words, but it would behoove us to prove to him that we can stop this thing before he takes other actions."

"Such as?"

"Don't ask, Ray. You don't want to hear it. Just get a report from Stuart and have him shut this thing down. Give him whatever he needs. I mean whatever he needs."

Carr nodded.

"I have to brief the boss again in three hours," Norman continued. "I'd really like to give him something concrete by then."

"I'm already working on it," Carr said.

"I know. Keep at it." The director left a confused Raymond Carr standing in his office.

Carr blinked. Other actions? What other actions?

8

Four hours later, Stuart dialed Carr's number from a pay phone on the second floor of the Ole Miss student union. He jammed the receiver between his shoulder and left ear while he rummaged through a small notebook, mentally organizing his information.

Carr came on the line almost immediately after a secretary had put Stuart on hold.

"How are you?" Carr said.

Stuart detected the stress in his voice. "Everything's good, so far," he said. "I just came from Moreland's office. He did it."

"No surprise there," Carr said. "As you can imagine, things are pretty tense here."

"Yeah, I figured."

"It's getting pretty dicey, Wade," Carr said. "We're overwhelmed at the moment and we're getting our information from CNN—until just now."

Stuart ignored the slight. "I can e-mail you a report in a couple of hours," he said. "It'll take me that long to get it all down. I've got enough to take Moreland down, if you can get me a task force to take out the militia compound."

"I'll take the report," Carr said, "but there's not going to be any task force."

"What?" Stuart's anger rose.

"The director just got off the phone with the President."

"Carr, there's no way I knew this was going to happen."

"Well, what happened?"

"They had it planned for a long time, according to Moreland," Stuart said. He briefly explained the operation.

"Damn," Carr said. "They put our asses in a sling on this one."

"What do you mean?"

Carr sighed. "The President, after he finished screaming at Norman, told him to forget about the task force we had planned. He called the Secretary of Defense and the Chairman of the Joint Chiefs and told them to prepare the Second Marine Division for deployment to Mississippi."

"He did what?" Stuart screamed. "How in the hell does he think he can get away with that? Has he lost his fucking mind?"

"Posse Comitatus is repealed, remember?" Carr said. "He can use federal troops in law-enforcement matters, just like he wanted to when he recommended repealing the law. Now he has the opportunity, and he's going one step further. He's going to declare the MPM a threat to the national security, a domestic enemy, which requires the use of the Marines."

Stuart grew cold in the dark hallway as he gripped the phone now, his hands sweaty. "That's insane," he said. "Those rednecks aren't a threat to national security. They're a ragtag bunch of idiots brainwashed by Moreland. It'll be a bloodbath. The public will never support it."

"Well, we'll see," Carr said. "The President is making a nation-wide speech to explain it to the country in just a few minutes. You near a TV?"

"Holy shit," Stuart said, ignoring the question. "Moreland's going to kill me as soon as he sees that speech. Carr, you have to do something."

"Like what? Disobey the President of the United States?"

"No, buy me some time," Stuart said. "Look, I'm going to make another weapons buy tonight. While I'm gone, can you at least call the Jackson office and set up a meeting between me and them? Let me talk to them and see if I can come up with a plan to at least arrest Moreland if nothing else."

The silence in Stuart's ear told him Carr was considering it.

"Come on, you owe me at least that much," Stuart said. "I'm running out of time, especially if the President's going on TV tonight."

"Okay, you got it," Carr said. "Where do you want to meet?" Stuart thought for a moment. "The Coast is the only place I feel safe. How about Biloxi?"

"Sure. The Jackson office is two agents," Carr said.

"Fine. Tell them to meet me at eight o'clock at mile marker 108 on Highway 90 East."

"Okay. What's there?" Carr said.

"A small dirt road," Stuart said. "Looks almost abandoned. It's right after the mile marker, on the right. Tell them to take the road for about half a mile—they'll be going toward the water—until they get to a clearing on the left. They'll see it. I'll meet them there. Got it?"

"Yes," Carr said. "Anything else?"

"No, that's it," Stuart said.

"Be careful."

"Better believe it," Stuart said as he hung.

Stuart glanced at his watch as he sat on an overstuffed chair in the union common area. He still had two hours before he had to make the trip to the Coast, and he wanted to see the President speak. He focused his attention on the small television perched on a raised shelf in the common area. A small group of students gathered below the television, their heads tilted upward, waiting.

The usual murmur of students in the union vanished as the President's face appeared on screen.

"My fellow Americans," the President said into the multitude of television cameras in the White House Briefing Room. "I come to you tonight to address the gravest of issues, and that is the butchery and terrorism that is taking place in our country."

The president provided an overview of the threat to the nation posed by the terrorists in Mississippi and the other radical groups nationwide, using the Jackson bombing as the centerpiece of this threat assessment. Behind the podium, he looked comfortable, almost fatherly.

Stuart watched the television slack-jawed, captivated as the President spoke.

"These acts of terrorism," the President said, "constitute an act of war and are unlike any other such acts in our history, even our own Civil War. This war is truly about the freedom of Americans, present and future. It is a war that comes to us not from faraway shores with unfamiliar names, but from within our own cities and towns.

"This very night, Americans are living in fear for their very lives against an evil—murderers that are running loose in the South tonight claiming that they launched their campaign of brutality in the name of freedom for all Americans. My friends, that is a lie. These thugs are trampling the very freedom they claim they are protecting. They cannot be considered Americans. They must be exposed for what they truly are, and that is traitors.

"Americans who oppose these cowards are the true freedom-loving Americans. As your President, I promise you this: the treason being perpetrated in the South will not stand.

"Tonight, I signed an executive order that will alert the Second Marine Division from Camp Lejeune, North Carolina, for possible deployment to Mississippi. To the citizens of Mississippi I say help is on the way. However, I ask for restraint on your part. To those of you who may be considering taking up arms, either against the so-called militiamen or against the military, I ask that you allow the Marines to do their jobs, if that time comes. Assist these troops in any way you can. I realize the difficulty this will cause many of you, but I ask that you think of the future of the nation, and allow our military to complete its mission as rapidly as possible.

"And to the murderers in the state of Mississippi, I say only this: cease your cowardly terrorism immediately or you will be destroyed."

The President pronounced the last few words slowly. The effect was profound. His words hung in the air of the White House Briefing Room and millions of homes across the country.

Immediately, an anchorman's perfectly coiffured head appeared on screen with an analysis of the speech, along with a self-proclaimed military expert, the latter of which caused Stuart to snort derisively. He tuned the television out as he watched the reactions of the students around him. Most seemed stunned. They wore looks of confusion and whispered urgently among themselves. Some shook their heads in disbelief as they walked away in pairs or in small groups.

Stuart knew better than to base an opinion of the public opinion on the reaction of a few college students, but he was struck with the shock he saw on their faces.

A hundred contradictory questions assaulted his brain. Was this truly a threat to the national security? Would Marines fire on fellow Americans?

Stuart recalled the oath of office to which he swore several years earlier as a Marine officer, "...defend the Constitution of the United States against all enemies, foreign and domestic..."

Domestic enemies. Was the MPM a legitimate domestic enemy—or a bunch of homicidal lunatics? Stuart admitted to himself that he didn't really know, regardless of what he had told Carr moments earlier. And if he didn't know, he knew full well that an eighteen-year-old private first class in a Marine Corps infantry company wouldn't.

He recalled something related to this very situation a couple of years earlier. A survey of Marines by some yahoo working on a master's thesis. The survey had included a question which asked Marines if they would fire on fellow Americans for refusing to give up their guns, even if Congress passed a law which authorized to do so. Stuart didn't know the results of that survey, something he longed to know now.

The way he had seen it then, no decent American serviceman would fire a weapon at another law-abiding American simply expressing his right to bear arms.

On the other hand, every member of the American military swore an oath to defend the Constitution of the United States—not the President—against all enemies, foreign and domestic. And if the MPM was a domestic enemy, then to refuse to fight would be an act of outright mutiny. The Civil War had already shown that there was such a thing as a domestic enemy, when Abraham Lincoln sent the U.S. Army into Virginia. What was the difference? Where was the line?

It had been a hotly debated topic on talk radio, along with topics such as the United Nations, the New World Order, militias and gun control, all of which were wrapped up in one conspiracy theory or another.

There were many groups in the country who had already seized upon this incident—the MPM was one—as just one more example of the government's attempts to subvert the Constitution, especially the Second Amendment. Although most of the groups were established hate groups like the Ku Klux Klan or the Aryan Nations, the emergence of the militias had troubled Stuart most. In fact, that concern was what caused Stuart to take this assignment.

As Stuart watched the post-address analysis, he remembered a few conversations he had with the Marine public affairs officer who had briefed him on the survey.

Captain Richard Hawkins had endured phone calls and letters from hundreds of angry citizens, from the rational to the kooky. He had even gone on several California talk radio shows to dispel the rumors that his base was training Marines to invade private homes and confiscate guns.

Stuart had paid close attention to the callers on several such radio shows. The issue of gun control stirred up violent emotions in the callers—egged on by the hosts. Congress, the media and the President were all blamed as Americans groped for a target for their frustration and fear.

A common theme, Stuart had noticed then, was that the government was doing its best to take away the rights of citizens to keep and bear arms at precisely the same time that violent crime was rampant in the streets—and getting worse. Many callers railed against Congress for doing nothing to stop the growing number of terrorist incidents in the country except trying to ban guns.

Stuart had agreed with Hawkins that this angry, scared segment of the national population was a critical element to the growing militia.

Now, the implications of that survey were coming to fruition and that prospect chilled Stuart. It was no longer an academic question. Marines would soon have to decide if they would fire upon armed Americans, decide if they would truly defend the Constitution against all enemies. It was a nightmare.

Stuart could sense that at Camp Lejeune, North Carolina, Marines were already trying to decide where their loyalties lay— with their president, their constitution, or their beliefs.

Stuart seriously wondered if the President had gone completely off the deep end. He was handing the radical right wing everything on a plate.

He glanced at his watch. He still had to e-mail Carr and meet with Moreland before driving to Electric Mills. He sighed as he hoisted himself up and headed for his car.

The meeting with Moreland was short, although Stuart was forced to endure another tirade from him. Stuart's mind surged with conflict as Moreland informed him that he had been in contact with other militias across the country, all of whom were mobilizing.

"For years now, the federal government has been easing the military into the civilian population," Moreland growled. "Disaster relief, riot control, law-enforcement assistance, you name it. The whole thing is a setup for a military occupation."

Stuart kept his mouth shut.

Eventually, they came to the subject of the weapons distribution. Moreland told Stuart that Sheriff Gage would assist him.

Stuart noticed that Moreland seemed preoccupied, but discounted it as anger over the president's speech and the news reports from Jackson. When Stuart pressed him for details about the recipients of the weapons, Moreland dismissed him with a wave.

"Tom will have all that," Moreland said. "Meet him at the jail when you leave here."

Stuart nodded and turned to go. Moreland called him back, and Stuart noticed Moreland's odd expression. He'd never seen Moreland with such a menacing, penetrating stare.

"You better start planning to hit the governor real soon," he said.

Stuart looked at Moreland for a long moment, nodded, then quickly left the room.

9

Stuart tried to sleep late after returning from Electric Mills at four in the morning. He was, however, too keyed up from the President's speech and its implications. He had also been irritated that Moreland wanted to have yet another meeting, this one about planning the governor's assassination. That meeting would be held at the militia compound in twenty-four hours.

Stuart's mind kept nagging at him that the entire situation was his fault. If he had known about the plans to bomb the courthouse, the President wouldn't have gone ballistic.

And if worms carried pistols, birds wouldn't fuck with them, Stuart thought, angry with himself. He fumed as he made coffee and breakfast. He was often mad at himself, and he knew it was because he was too much of a perfectionist. And knowing that only made him angrier. He also knew he was letting his temper control his actions and cloud his judgment, which was dangerous for an undercover agent, especially one whose cover was hanging by a thread.

He sat and forced himself to calm down as he sipped coffee. He felt alone. He stared at the wall, then at his apartment. He felt a deep, sad loneliness as he realized that his whole adult life had been spent in moments such as this—facing a crisis, facing death in fact, alone and overwhelmed. It's enough, he thought, to drive a man to despair. He had felt the coldness before, the black cocoon of fear that always seemed to prompt a longing for companionship.

It never goes away, he thought.

Stuart considered calling Lee Ann, but gave up. Dragging her into this was not only stupid, it was dangerous. Ironic, he thought, he finally had the chance to find that companionship, but if he did it was even more dangerous.

He moved to the living room and turned on the television. An information junkie, Stuart tuned to CNN as hungrily as a smoker going for a cigarette.

Now he knew how people got hooked on CNN during Desert Storm, he thought as he listened to yet another update on the possible deployment of the Second Marine Division.

CNN aired a special report from Camp Lejeune, North Carolina. He watched B-roll of base housing and barracks as a reporter explained the preparations now going on.

Stuart went for more coffee as the reporter seemed determined to convey the entire history of the division to the public, from World War II to the present.

When he returned, he saw footage of M1A1 main battle tanks rolling through the dusty sands of Kuwait during Desert Storm. He noticed that not much was mentioned about Beirut, a city he and the Second Marine Division were familiar with.

The on-screen view then shifted to inside an office, then Stuart was face-to-face with the commander of the Second Marine Division. From his spacious office in an imposing two-story red brick building which housed the division headquarters, Major General Jack Conklin glared at the three-inch-thick document on the desk in front of him. Stuart realized this was more B-roll as the reporter began another voice-over, this time providing a detailed biography of the general.

Jack Conklin had been a Marine officer for twenty-seven years, the reporter said. Except for the years since his promotion to the rank of brigadier general, Conklin had been an infantryman.

Stuart had known Conklin in his Marine Corps days and thought him to be a gifted leader and thoroughly professional warrior. His grasp of tactics, strategy, and the subtleties of geopolitics was far better than most officers.

If a division of Marines had to come here, he's the right man for the job, Stuart thought. The old man must be agonizing over this one.

Stuart remembered the numerous times Conklin had preached to junior officers that each time he entered combat, he was struck by how different it was from the last time. This realization, and especially his Vietnam experience, caused him to vow that he would not become afflicted with the malady of many senior U.S. military officers—fighting the last war in the current one. He had seen far too many people killed because of the simple fact that what applied in the last war didn't apply in this one. Stuart hoped the general remembered those sermons in a few weeks.

The news report cut to a shot of the reporter in a parking lot, surrounded by long lines of huge pallets of Marine Corps gear. The division, the reporter explained, would move in segments, with tanks and amphibious-assault vehicles aboard flatbed trucks. Personnel would be transported in humvees, trucks, helicopters, and C-130 cargo planes.

"Commanders here say Marine aviation would provide the much-needed protection to the supply line," the reporter said. "The AV-8B Harrier jet, with its vertical and short-takeoff capability and the impressive payload of bombs it could deliver to a target, will be the workhorse of the operation."

The report cut abruptly back to Conklin's face, which Stuart thought looked much older than when he had last seen the general in person.

"Of course, we hope for a more reasonable resolution to the militia situation in Mississippi," Conklin said to the reporter. "But we also follow the orders of the Commander in Chief. And we're ready."

The reporter signed off, and Stuart turned the television off. He thought about the oath of office, and felt doubt once again. That oath had been really bothering him lately. Could he do what those Marines were going to have to do? He wasn't sure.

Stuart remembered a similar crisis of conscience from his college days, when he first confronted the paradox of defending Americans he despised.

It was his senior year, 1983, when he had seen firsthand the destructiveness of the hatred Moreland displayed. In fact, that hate had been part of the reason why he had left Mississippi. That year, he had watched helplessly as racism became the centerpiece of the Ole Miss campus.

The university had been challenged by a black student over the issue of something Stuart had not really put much thought into: the Confederate battle flag.

For many years, Ole Miss students—who were overwhelmingly white—had waved small "Rebel flags" at football games instead of pompoms commonly seen in stadiums. Stuart had owned one himself, along with a five-foot by seven-foot version which hung in his dormitory room.

He had always gotten a thrill seeing thousands of flags snapping in the fall breeze, so many that the faces of the fans below them all but disappeared.

But he never thought the flag was a symbol of racism. True, he reasoned, it represented the Confederacy in the War Between the States, but that was a long time ago. Today, the flag was nothing more than a symbol of school spirit, just as many of the white students claimed.

Or so he had thought.

Stuart remembered the "spirit campaign" started by white students to show that the Confederate flag was nothing more than a symbol of the Ole Miss student spirit.

One day during the campaign, four extremely drunken fraternity boys careened around campus in a Jeep festooned with Rebel flags. The frat brothers were also decked out, with flags draped over their shoulders or tied around their heads.

As they screamed, "Save the flag!" and honked the horn, passers-by gave them the half-smile and glance usually reserved for drunken fools.

Stuart had been descending a small hill in the center of campus when the group rattled past him. Then, a few yards ahead, he saw a black female student walking on the sidewalk. Before Stuart could react, the Jeep lurched recklessly to the sidewalk. The whiskey-fueled men glared at the girl through barely focused eyes. She stopped, glanced to her sides, then tried to continue her walk.

"Go home, nigger!" one frat boy screamed.

Traffic stopped. Students snapped their heads in the direction of the Jeep. The girl looked humiliated—at first. Stuart sprinted toward her. As he did, he saw her expression—resolute, hard and hating.

Now the other frat boys joined in.

"Yeah, nigger, go home! Save the flag!"

Laughing and hooting, the group shot away from the curb as the driver released the clutch. Stuart reached the girl's side just in time to hear her mutter, "Bastards."

All doubt about the meaning of the flag was erased a few weeks later. Even as white students maintained the silly premise that it represented school spirit, people took sides along race. Black students—if they went to class at all—walked in groups. They staged rallies and sang, "We Shall Overcome."

Then, on a crisp fall Saturday morning, the phone in Stuart's dorm room rang. It was a friend, telling him in nervous excited tones to get to Oxford's town square.

The Ku Klux Klan was in town.

Stuart made it to the square just as the lead element of a Klan parade turned off Jackson Avenue into the square. Several hundred onlookers, including about fifty blacks, gawked silently at the white sheets moving menacingly down the street.

Every Klansman carried a Confederate flag.

Stuart turned his back to the scene in anger and revulsion. He simply could not believe what he was witnessing. He had been forced to think about the meaning of the flag, and now he saw it for what it was. A vicious, insulting symbol of racial hate.

Although several of his ancestors had fought under that flag, he wished he had never seen one. The thrill of seeing thousands of those flags at football games was replaced with shame with seeing them in the hands of the Ku Klux Klan.

Stuart had walked slowly back to his dorm that day, head down, tears occasionally falling to the sidewalk as he realized that the passage of time had done nothing to erase the destructive power of racism.

That night, he had decided to take in a basketball game. As he walked to the coliseum, he noticed yet another gathering of students, this time in the grove facing the Lyceum, the stately old administration building. Two hundred white students had gathered for another rally.

Curious, Stuart stopped at the edge of the crowd to watch. On the steps of the Lyceum, a student made his way to a small, portable podium with a microphone. Behind the crowd stood a flagpole.

The student grabbed the microphone, ostensibly to show the flag was nothing more than a symbol of school spirit.

"Nigger go home!" the student shouted.

The words echoed across the cool campus night. Stuart stared dumbfounded at the Lyceum as the chant was picked up by the crowd.

Then a pair of students ran to the flagpole, loosened the halyard and hauled down the United States flag. One of the boys grabbed the flag, removed it and affixed the Confederate flag. It was hauled to the top of the pole amid the lusty cheers of the crowd.

Stuart stood, angry and shocked. He turned his back and fought back tears of shame as the crowd roared its approval.

It was a mockery. A mockery of the American flag. He had decided to risk his life to defend that flag—this nation—and two people had just run up a Confederate flag where only an American flag should fly.

I'm supposed to defend these people, he had thought bitterly.

Stuart had moved quickly to his dorm. He had wanted to be

away from the scene as fast as possible, away from the embarrassment, away from the spoiled rich white kids who were as hateful and racist as their rich parents.

When he returned to his room, he snatched the Confederate flag from the wall. He vented his anger by tearing the flag to shreds and flinging the pieces out the ninth-floor window.

Now, more than a dozen years later, Stuart felt as if that issue was arising again.

I'm right back where I started, he thought as the images from the news reports tumbled over his memories like waves over a rocky beach. Watching hate tear this state apart. I've got to stop Moreland before those Marines deploy.

That evening, after dark, Stuart pulled to the shoulder of Highway 90 east of Biloxi. Although a busy highway day and night, Stuart drew little attention from motorists as his car slowed near the dirt road on the right shoulder.

Stuart killed the engine, then walked down the dark road. His .45 was in the small of his back, tucked into the waistband of his jeans. On his left hip, under a bulky sweatshirt, he wore his .357 Magnum revolver, with the butt facing forward so he could cross-draw the weapon. In his right hip pocket were his ATF credentials, along with four high-density three-and-a-half-inch computer diskettes containing all the information on his investigation.

Stuart felt like a federal agent again.

When he had gone about two hundred yards, he heard his name called out in a low voice.

Shit, Stuart thought, I've got to pay more attention.

He had expected to be the first to arrive, but he didn't show his surprise. He turned to face the ATF agent from Jackson. He saw that the man was holding something in his right hand. As Stuart walked toward him, he recognized the familiar peculiar shape of night vision glasses.

The agent offered his hand and Stuart shook it.

"Thought you were bringing another agent with you," Stuart

said, more out of curiosity than suspicion.

A second agent stepped onto the road.

"Evening, Stuart," he said. "Special Agent Leonard Everett."

"And I'm Robert Chandler," said the man in front of Stuart. He expertly flashed his credentials. Everett did the same.

"Nice to meet you," Stuart said as he reached for the diskettes. "Guess you knew it was me coming down the road."

Chandler smiled and said, "They told us to look for a guy needing a haircut and built like a cornerback. You're the only person fitting that description that's come down the road tonight."

Stuart chuckled. He handed the diskettes to Chandler.

"That's it," Stuart said. "Quick and simple. Now all I need you to do is take a look at that data—quickly—and see if the three of us can come up with some sort of plan to shut this militia down before the Marines have to come do it."

Chandler grinned. "That's what you call quick and simple? Don't worry, we'll take a look at it as soon as we get back," he said. "Washington told us to accommodate you any way we could, as long as we did it quietly. You know we're officially off the investigation?"

"Yeah," Stuart said. "Carr told me."

"Okay," Chandler said. "Did you make copies of the disks?"

"Didn't have time. I don't need copies. Believe me, I'm intimately familiar with all the info."

Chandler laughed. "Yeah, I bet you are. Give you a lift?"

"No, thanks. My car's just up the road."

"Okay, Everett and I will be on our way. Good luck. Be careful."

"I will."

Chandler stepped off to join Everett. Stuart watched him disappear, then walked briskly to his car. He still had to get back to Bedford and get some sleep before meeting with Moreland the next morning.

10

Camp Lejeune, North Carolina, consists of two hundred and forty-six square miles of swampy tidewater coast that can be equally miserable in the summer or winter. Nestled against the community of Jacksonville, the base was carved out of the Carolina swamp in the days prior to World War II.

The base is the headquarters for numerous commands, including the Second Marine Division. The division, part of the forty-three thousand active-duty garrison at the base and part of the II Marine Expeditionary Force, serves as the ground combat element, or "fighting arm" of II MEF.

The division was officially established February 1, 1941, at Camp Elliot, California, near Kearny Mesa. With war in the Pacific looming, the division grew quickly and trained steadily for the war that, for the United States, began at Pearl Harbor.

In November 1943, the division stormed ashore at a tiny speck of Pacific sand called Tarawa. The three-day battle, in which nine hundred and eighty-four Marines were killed and another two thousand seventy-two were wounded, was one of the bloodiest in American history.

The division went on to play an integral role in America's amphibious war in the Pacific, fighting gallantly at Saipan, Tinian and Okinawa.

When the war was over, the division returned Stateside and settled into Camp Lejeune. The unit would not deploy again as a division for nearly fifty years.

With the onset of the Cold War, the division's focus was the Atlantic, Europe and the Caribbean. When the North Koreans invaded their kinsmen to the south in 1950, First Marine Division answered the call. Second Marine Division continued its mission of months-long deployments aboard naval ships to potential hot spots such as the Mediterranean.

During the 1950s, units from the division deployed to Beirut, Lebanon, and the Dominican Republic to protect U.S. interests and support these countries' governments.

During the Vietnam War, First and Third Marine Divisions deployed and fought in the jungles, while Second Marine Division continued its role in Cold War deterrence.

In the 1980s, Second Marine Division units participated in the ill-fated multinational peacekeeping mission in Beirut which ended tragically when an Islamic fundamentalist drove an explosives-laden truck into the Marine barracks, leveling the entire building and killing more than two hundred Marines and sailors while they slept.

Units also participated in the brief but sharp campaign to free American medical students in the Caribbean nation of Grenada. The Marine Amphibious Unit, the manifestation of the Reagan Doctrine, routed the Grenadine army much in the same manner that a bear swats flies.

Over the years, a rivalry understandably developed between the Marines of Second Marine Division and their brother Marines of the First Division on the West Coast. The Second Division, not without some help from what the First Marine Division dubbed the "East Coast Mafia," portrayed itself as the "tip of the spear" of national defense.

It was therefore understandable that a chuckle could be heard floating across the hills of Camp Pendleton, California, in August 1990, when the First Marine Division, as part of I Marine Expeditionary Force, was ordered to deploy to the Kingdom of Saudi Arabia in response to Iraqi dictator Saddam Hussein's invasion of Kuwait.

Frustration mounted among the officers and men of Second Marine Division as the weeks passed. Being Marines trained to be the "first to fight," they felt as if they were being benched during the big game.

That is, until the President of the United States ordered more troops into the region, and the Second Marine Division prepared to mount out.

The Marines already in the desert were unable to see most of the media coverage of Second Division's deployment, but they did hear the comments of the Commandant of the Marine Corps as he visited troops preparing to deploy.

The general said, on camera, that he was "sending in the 'A-team' now."

This comment raised more than a few eyebrows in the First Marine Division, and more than one Marine was known to have snorted and said, "What the hell are we—chopped liver?" One running joke among the First Division Marines was that the Marine Corps would have the largest intramural firefight in history once the Second Marine Division arrived.

This, of course, did not happen, and rivalry or not, both divisions performed superbly in the rout and destruction of the Iraqi army.

After the Persian Gulf War concluded, the Second Marine Division returned to Camp Lejeune to resume the somewhat mundane routine of training for six-month deployments to the Mediterranean, Norway or other areas at sea.

The division's "tip of the spear" image took another blow when the First Marine Division was called on again, this time in 1992, to deploy to the anarchy of Somalia.

In 1994, the lead element of the 1st Marine Division deployed once again to Kuwait in response to threatening movements by Iraq's rejuvenated army.

So, as word spread that the Second Marine Division was about to deploy to Mississippi, many Camp Lejeune Marines secretly and smugly snickered at their fortune. Many of them, especially senior-ranking officers and enlisted men who had spent the majority of their careers in North Carolina, thought it was high time the Second Division got an opportunity to show what it could do alone, and not hanging on the coattails of those Hollywood bastards at Pendleton.

The commander of the Second Marine Division, however, did not share this sentiment, nor was he even remotely concerned about the First Marine Division at the moment. He had many other matters to contend with.

From his office in the division headquarters, Major General Jack Conklin glared at the three-inch-thick document on the desk in front of him.

The document was the operations order for the division's deployment. His concern at the moment was the protection of the massive convoy that would soon make its way along the highways across the heart of the Deep South.

Conklin had no illusions about the "alert." He knew his division would deploy soon. Even if it didn't, he would be damned sure that it was able to.

The division would move in segments, with tanks and amphibious assault vehicles aboard flatbed trucks. Personnel would be transported in humvees, trucks, helicopters, C-130 cargo planes, and any other form of transportation that could be found.

Conklin knew these segments could count on flank security during movement from the division's Light Armored Reconnaissance Battalion mounted in LAV-25s, potent eight-wheeled armored vehicles. The same was true for the follow-on logistical convoys which would follow.

The general was not exceptionally worried about actually getting his division into the state. His main concern was keeping that Mississippi-North Carolina supply line open once it was in place.

General Sherman must have worried about the same thing down here, Conklin thought wryly.

Like that Union general who plowed through Georgia, Conklin faced the potential for predatory raids on his supply lines and rear areas, raids which could be anything from merely bothersome to catastrophic.

Unlike Sherman, however, Conklin possessed one capability that gave him great comfort. He could rely upon Marine aviation overhead providing the much-needed protection to his rear units. The Marine Corps inventory could handle just about any contingency. II MEF's air component, Second Marine Aircraft Wing, contained attack, transport, and command and control helicopters, as well as fighter, attack, reconnaissance, and cargo fixed-wing aircraft. The AV-8B "Harrier" jet, Conklin figured, would be the workhorse of this operation, with its vertical and short takeoff capability and the impressive payload of bombs it could deliver to a target.

What bothered Conklin was the fact that Second MAW's primary mission would be to provide support to the combat troops actually doing the fighting, not the supply routes, and rightly so. Conklin fervently hoped that the air assets would be available whenever he needed them for support in the rear, but he knew better than to expect that. The operations order, which his own staff drafted, clearly spelled out the priorities of Second MAW.

Conklin pushed the op order away and sighed. He'd have to do the best he could. He stood and walked to the large window in his office.

He gazed at the vast rectangular parade deck, brown and denuded by fall, that stretched before him and thought about the mission he may soon undertake.

Jack Conklin had been a grunt his entire adult life. He graduated from Oregon State University in 1967. By 1968, he was a second lieutenant commanding a platoon in a little piece of hell called Khe Sanh. He was at the besieged outpost near South Vietnam's De-Militarized Zone from start to finish, and watched every man in his platoon, himself included, get wounded or killed.

Conklin received the Silver Star for his bravery at Khe Sanh, specifically for leading a counterattack against a much larger

North Vietnamese Army force which had overrun his position. Grievously wounded in the right leg by a mortar blast, Conklin was thought dead.

Conklin, however, rose up on the mangled limb, rallied his men, and drove the enemy back down the hill the enemy had attacked. Conklin himself killed five NVA troops with an entrenching tool, the only weapon he could find after his rifle was shattered by the mortar blast which wounded him.

When Conklin returned from Vietnam, doctors recommended he be medically retired because of his wounds. Conklin, now a brand-new captain, fought the doctors vehemently. He demanded to be allowed to remain on active duty, even though he knew that refusing medical retirement would cost him any medical benefits to which he might be entitled upon his regular retirement. Conklin was allowed to remain on active duty.

His superiors saw that Conklin was a gifted leader and thoroughly professional warrior. His grasp of tactics, strategy, and the subtleties of geopolitics was far better than most officers.

This recognition of his talents was evident in his fitness reports and duty stations, which indicated that Conklin was being "groomed" for a general's star. At each level of rank, Conklin always surpassed his peers and even those who were his "superiors."

Now, three months away from turning fifty, the general thought about this as he stared out the window and felt the weight of ten thousand men and women on his shoulders. As he thought about his Marines, he grinned to himself at the nickname they had given him, though few Marines had any idea Conklin knew it.

The division staff had secretly dubbed Conklin "Rattler" shortly after he assumed the duties as division commander. This was because of a characteristic the general usually displayed at staff meetings, particularly in the field.

Conklin had a habit of hunching down in his chair while listening to staff officers give their briefs. With his chin nearly on his chest and his eyelids half-closed, Conklin looked almost sleepy, or, as one major remarked, like a rattler about to strike. Conklin could indeed strike like a rattlesnake. His demeanor was deceptive, especially to the unfortunate staff officer who approached the podium or map unprepared and tried to bluff his way through a brief. At the instant Conklin sensed this was happening, he would lash out viciously at the briefer. Conklin would snap upright in his chair and deliver a blistering denunciation of the officer's lack of preparation, knowledge or professionalism. The general's tongue was often so acerbic that the officer who was the target of the tongue-lashing truly felt as if he'd been bitten by a rattlesnake.

Although Conklin did nothing to encourage his Marines to call him "Rattler," he didn't discourage it, either. If he had the reputation among his troops of being a man they couldn't bullshit, he could live with it.

"Hey sleepyhead," Lee Ann whispered into Stuart's ear.

Stuart grumbled a response into the cordless phone, then glanced at the nightstand clock.

"Lee Ann," he said. "It's six o'clock."

"I know," she said. "I'm getting dressed for class and thought I'd give you a wake-up call." She giggled.

Stuart smiled. He climbed out of bed and went into the kitchen.

"Are we still on for tonight?" she asked as Stuart made a pot of coffee.

"Huh? Oh, yeah, six-thirty, right?" Stuart remembered that he and Lee Ann had a date that night in Oxford. Lee Ann was taking a full course load this semester and wanted a break from her studies.

"Yes. I have reservations for seven o'clock."

"Okay. I'll pick you up at the dorm at six-thirty."

"See you then," Lee Ann said, then hung up. Stuart grumbled as he poured himself a cup of coffee and pondered breakfast. He still had two hours before his meeting with Moreland.

What the hell, he thought. He decided to drive to the compound anyway. He could kill time checking the perimeter.

As Stuart ascended the hill leading to the compound, he listened to the gravel crunching under his tires and contemplated Moreland's odd mood the previous day. At first, he dismissed it as anger, but it seemed more than that. Moreland appeared to be holding something back and at the same time seemed vaguely threatening. Stuart wondered if Moreland was plotting another bombing. It wouldn't be surprising, considering the rage he had displayed two days earlier.

Stuart crossed the barbed wire perimeter and into the open area between the militia's buildings. At the far end of the quad, outside the building which housed Moreland's office, Stuart saw a group of men standing together. Curious as to why anyone other than Amos Moreland was here at this early hour, Stuart looked closely as he drove to the building.

As he drew nearer, he recognized Gage, Tanner and Moreland, who stood with two other men. Tanner loosely held an M16A2. The three were intently watching Stuart with a look of near surprise.

The trio stood with the two ATF agents with whom Stuart had met the night before.

The realization hit Stuart so quickly he had no time to think, except for the thought that he had been masterfully set up. He jammed on his brakes and yanked his .45 from the small of his back.

The sudden stop of the car caused the five men to jump into action as if they had each received an electric shock. The impostor agents reached into their coats and produced Uzi submachine guns. Tanner, an arrogant smile on his face, slowly raised his rifle.

Stuart was already moving, watching the scene as if it were in slow motion. With his left hand, he spun the steering wheel as he hit the accelerator. He fired through the passenger-side window.

His first round shattered the glass, but Stuart did not hear the sound. He slowed the car enough to send the group diving for cover with a fusillade of pistol fire. One bullet found its mark, hitting one of the impostors in the chest and toppling him.

Stuart raced out of the compound toward the highway, cursing and trembling from an adrenaline rush, but thinking clearly. He saw plumes of dirt erupt alongside his car. He heard and felt several bullets from the remaining Uzi slam into his car.

The whole operation was blown. The agents had been sent by Moreland, that was obvious. The question was, how had they known about the meeting?

The tires screeched as Stuart's car hit the pavement and fishtailed. He fought the car back under control and gunned the engine. He checked his rearview mirror. There were no pursuers—yet. He knew, however, that in a very short time he would be pursued by Moreland and company. And shot, if caught.

Obviously, the phone line at the Jackson ATF office had been tapped, Stuart thought. No one else but Stuart and the Jackson agents—the real ones—knew about the meeting.

They're probably dead, Stuart thought. And if they are, ATF would be screaming its head off by now. What the hell is going on in Washington?

As he headed toward Bedford at over ninety miles per hour, his mind reeled off an inventory of his apartment. As the kudzu-covered landscape whipped by, he decided that to return there would be useless—and dangerous. He carried his .45—the thought reminded him to change magazines as soon as he had a chance—and, in an ankle holster, the .357. Ammunition was in the trunk, along with an M16A2 rifle and a bandoleer of ammo. His cellular phone was in the glove compartment, along with a Marine Corps fighting knife. He even had a set of NVGs and binoculars, and plenty of cash.

A glance in the rearview mirror revealed his pursuers, still distant, but closing. When Stuart saw flashing lights, he realized that Gage, in his official vehicle, would surely radio his deputies and the highway patrol to set up a roadblock.

Stuart's breathing quickened. He had to get out of this county before that could happen.

Lee Ann.

Stuart caught sight of a dirt road ahead, bisecting a soybean field. He jerked the wheel and steered the car off the pavement. If he could only make it to Oxford, he could talk to Lee Ann and convince her to help him. Or could he?

Either way, paranoid or not, Stuart figured he had no choice. The dirt path ended abruptly and Stuart nearly sailed over a two-lane county road. He grappled with the wheel and pointed the car east, toward Oxford. He didn't even bother to look behind him. He knew they were there. But, if he was lucky, he had a fifty-fifty chance if the militiamen chose the wrong direction.

He punched the glove compartment open and grabbed a small cellular phone.

Raymond Carr answered his phone on the second ring.

"Carr."

"Stuart. Don't talk, just listen. I'm screwed."

"What? How?" Carr said.

"Best I can figure, the MPM tapped the Jackson office phone." Stuart paused. "Have you heard from Jackson?"

"No, why?"

"Chandler and Everett are most likely dead."

"What?" Carr asked.

Stuart told him about the set-up and his escape.

"Where are you now?" Carr said.

"On a back road heading east toward Oxford. I can meet someone there who'll probably help. But these guys are on my ass. I don't have a lot of time."

"I know. Look, get somewhere safe and call the nearest office. I'll put the word out right now," Carr said.

"Okay, but hurry. It's going to be real hard for me to move once Gage alerts the cops. I'm sure he'll put out an A.P.B. for me on an attempted murder charge."

"I know," Carr said again. "We'll get you back in."

"You better." Stuart broke the connection and stuffed the phone into his coat pocket.

He tore into Lafayette County on a quiet road that paralleled Highway 6 East, which led to Oxford. Only a few more miles, he thought, and he'd have some breathing room.

Stuart turned off Highway 6 onto Jackson Avenue, which led to the Ole Miss campus. So far, he had not been followed, nor had he seen a cop, but he knew it was only a matter of time.

He exceeded the speed limit as much as he dared through the outskirts of the small college town, past the bowling alley and fast-food restaurants. He turned left again into the parking lot of a mini-mall located just off campus. Stuart parked his car between several others and walked quickly into the Wal-Mart store at one end of the mall.

He emerged five minutes later with a large, dark blue backpack.

When he returned to his car, Stuart opened the trunk and began loading the backpack with his weapons. He checked the area for curious passers-by—or cops—and disassembled the rifle. He carefully stored the parts, wrapped in a towel he kept in the trunk, in the pack's main compartment, along with the ammunition and NVGs. The pistols went into side pockets.

After he stowed the weapons, Stuart reached under the spare tire and pulled out a small, flat leather case. He opened it and glanced at his ATF badge and identification.

No sense hiding these now, he thought. He shoved the badge into his coat pocket next to his cellular phone and closed the trunk.

After another scan of the area, Stuart locked the car and walked away, hoisting the pack on his shoulder.

The mall was located next to a thicket of tall pine trees. Stuart casually entered the woods and knelt, eyeing his car. He checked his watch. It was only 9:30. He had to contact Lee Ann, but he had no idea which class she was attending.

Stuart fretted. Walking around campus in broad daylight caused him some apprehension, but he reasoned he could probably blend in. He wore jeans and a leather jacket over a T-shirt, and with the backpack he looked like a college student. He considered making a trip to the Lyceum, the main administration building, to obtain a copy of Lee Ann's class schedule, but he doubted the school officials would comply, unless he flashed an ATF badge at them. That would cause many questions that Stuart was not willing to answer, however.

And, he thought as he watched the parking lot, he had to assume that Moreland had already guessed his destination and alerted the campus offices to be on the lookout for a man fitting his description asking for Lee Ann Weatherby.

A half hour passed. No one even came near the car. Satisfied he had not been followed, Stuart moved away through the woods. He crossed Jackson Avenue and climbed a steep embankment and re-entered a stand of trees. He worked his way around two dormitories and past a group of athletic fields to the athletic dorm. He broke out of the woods onto a street that led to the heart of the campus.

At first, he felt conspicuous as he walked between a row of old student dorms, as if everyone he met knew he wasn't really a student. It had been years since Stuart had walked these streets as an undergrad, and he felt a curious nostalgia with his nearly overwhelming apprehension.

In the peculiar fashion of students, each person Stuart met averted his or her eyes as Stuart approached. Some things never change, he thought and relaxed.

Stuart walked past the cafeteria, the haberdashery, and the Public Relations Department. On an impulse and in the hope of catching Lee Ann between classes, Stuart ducked into the massive three-story library.

He strolled through the lobby and down a darkened hallway which led into the reading room. As when he studied here, Stuart immediately noticed that more socializing was taking place than reading. The students maintained a loud buzz of conversation, paper rustling and walking about the expansive room filled with tables and chairs.

Stuart roved through the room, careful not to make eye contact or appear to be searching. A two-minute search told him Lee Ann was not there.

Stuart left the library and walked toward the student union building. He threaded his way through a throng of students between Fulton Chapel and the fine arts building, scanning each face for Lee Ann.

He entered the glass doors of the union and checked the snack bar before walking downstairs to the bookstore and post office, where most students spent their time in the union.

After a cursory reconnaissance of the bookstore, Stuart began checking the cubbyholes filled with student mailboxes. Each was crammed with students. Mounds of paper littered the floor.

At the second section, Stuart's pulse quickened. He saw Lee Ann. Her back faced him as she stooped to retrieve several pieces of mail. Stuart waited.

She turned and recognized him with a start.

"Wade! What are you doing here?" she said, smiling.

"Looking for you." Lee Ann's smile turned into a questioning look as Stuart took her firmly by the arm.

"We need to talk—now," Stuart said. "Hungry?"

Lee Ann nodded, and slipped her hand into Stuart's.

"Let's go upstairs," Stuart said.

Stuart led Lee Ann to a corner of the snack bar after they received their sandwiches.

"Wade, I don't know what to say. This is actually romantic," she said, giving Stuart a warm smile.

Stuart gazed at the beautiful woman and for an instant forgot about the madness around him. For a moment, he allowed himself to drink in the warmth and sensuality of the woman sitting across from him. But only for a moment.

"Lee Ann, listen," he said. "Something has happened and it

involves me and your uncle."

Lee Ann reached across the table and gently touched Stuart's hand. Stuart saw her eyes searching his, revealing her confusion and concern.

"Lee Ann, your Uncle Amos is involved in a militia," Stuart said. He told her about Moreland's involvement in the Jackson bombing.

Lee Ann snatched her hand from Stuart's as the color left her face, only to be replaced with crimson anger.

"Wade," she said. "What are you talking about? That's absolutely ridiculous!"

Stuart reached into his coat pocket, produced his badge and slid the case across the table.

"Lee Ann," he said, "I'm Special Agent Wade Stuart of the Bureau of Alcohol, Tobacco and Firearms. I was sent down here by Washington to work undercover because of information we received about possible militia activity in the state. Your uncle's name was one of the first ones I was given. Amos Moreland is the head—the commander—of the Mississippi People's Militia."

Stuart noticed the disbelieving look on Lee Ann's face. She trembled.

"Lee Ann, look, I know you don't want to believe it, but it's true."

"Believe it?" Lee Ann asked. She lowered her voice. "You liar. Why should I believe you? You've been lying to me all along. You knew I was Amos Moreland's niece and you used me."

Stuart, aghast, realized he had completely misread her earlier expression. "No," he said. "I did not. I never once lied to you about anything other than what I really do for a living. I had no idea you were even related to Moreland until you introduced me to him at that party. That's the truth."

"You expect me to believe that?" Lee Ann asked.

Stuart looked steadily at her. "Yes, I do," he said. "What's happened between us has nothing to do with this."

Lee Ann stared at Stuart for a long moment. "Okay, I believe you, but I still don't understand all this," she said with a doubtful look.

Stuart briefly told Lee Ann how he infiltrated the militia, bought weapons and trained the members. He was careful to avoid details and did not specify all that he knew about Amos Moreland.

"But they found out," Stuart said. "Somehow they found out I was an ATF agent and they set me up."

"How could they have known?" Lee Ann asked.

"I wish I knew," Stuart said. He had a feeling that Charlie Tanner was responsible, but he didn't tell Lee Ann. "But they did, and the whole thing blew up this morning. After you called, I couldn't sleep so I drove out to the MPM compound a little early. I surprised them. Then I had to take off. Which brings me here."

Lee Ann seemed frightened. "So they're chasing you?"

Stuart nodded. "I lost them. But it's only a matter of time. They'll alert every cop in the state to be looking out for me. That's why I came to you. I need your help, and I need to get you away from this, too. Sooner or later, they'll come to you. Everybody knows we've been seeing each other."

"What can I do?"

"For now, you can meet me at your dorm at five o'clock. That'll give me time to take care of some loose ends and make a couple of calls to Washington. Just make sure your car has plenty of gas."

Lee Ann nodded.

Stuart nodded back. "Good," he said. "I've got to get going. Don't come out of your dorm until exactly five o'clock. Then go to your car as fast as possible without being obvious. I'll be watching you the entire time."

Stuart's last words chilled Lee Ann; she realized for the first time the danger involved.

Stuart abruptly leaned across the table and kissed Lee Ann gently on the lips. Lee Ann returned the kiss with a fierceness that surprised and, in some odd way, comforted Stuart.

After he left, Lee Ann took a deep breath, collected her books and left for her next class.

In the Administration's brief history of three years, no one could recall a more explosive, or angrier, reaction to a brief by the President. Seated in the Pentagon's "Tank"—the Oval Office was too small for the brief and too inconvenient for the military attendees—were the President, the Secretary of Defense and the National Security Advisor, collectively known as the National Command Authority; the Vice President; the director of the CIA and his deputy; the Chairman and members of the Joint Chiefs of Staff; and all the underling attendants for men of such stature.

The director of the ATF stood nervously—almost ashamedly—at one end of the room next to a screen, upon which various slides relating to the current status of the Mississippi People's Militia had just been shown.

Charles Norman had noticed the President becoming more and more irritated during the course of his brief, which, admittedly, had almost sounded like one fuck-up after another.

When Norman finished, he was immediately greeted with a string of obscenities not heard from a President by anyone in the room for years. Hence, the director's nervousness.

"You mean to tell me," the President snarled in a manner that belied his Midwestern country-boy roots, "that you had a man in that militia weeks before the bombing, yet it took you by surprise?"

"Mr. President," the director said gamely before being cut off with a violent wave.

"By surprise. Just what the hell was this guy doing down there? Fishing? This is the most unbelievable thing I've ever heard! And, now you're telling me that this agent – who's done such a wonderful job until now—has had his cover blown, thereby practically guaranteeing that we'll never be able to pin anything on these murderers!"

The director inwardly relaxed. The President, however grudgingly, was beginning to sound more presidential. That meant he was calming down, albeit in stages.

"Not exactly, Mr. President," Norman said, smiling for the first time. "Before Special Agent Stuart's cover was blown, he sent us, via electronic mail, every piece of information he had on the MPM, to include digital photos and diagrams of the militia's compound.

"Well, at least we got something out of this fiasco," the President snapped.

Norman drew in his breath. "Mr. President, two agents have already died in this 'fiasco,' as you call it. Two of my agents. I can assure you that we are doing everything possible to arrest the leaders of the MPM as quickly as possible."

The reference to the dead ATF agents caused the President to rein in his anger. "I'm sorry about your men," he said. "But, as to your plans, I believe we have passed beyond simple criminal activity on the part of the Mississippi People's Militia."

Norman glanced at the impassive faces seated around the long, polished table. He noticed a flicker of emotion pass across the faces of the generals. The President began speaking to the room.

"Gentlemen, this group and many like it pose a grave risk to our domestic national security. Already, the MPM has succeeded in committing an act of terrorism on a government building with plans to assassinate the governor of Mississippi and eventually take control of the state. This will not happen.

"At this point, we don't know if the MPM is in collusion with other militias with similar plans," the President said.

Norman took the last statement personally. He was getting a cheap shot from the President of the United States.

"However," the President said, "we must assume two things: one, that they are, and two, that this group's actions and intentions could motivate other groups to do the same. Again, this cannot and will not happen. As President of the United States, I am prepared to end this insurrection by all means necessary."

At the word "insurrection" the Chairman of the Joint Chiefs of Staff shot a glance at the Commander-in-Chief. The Joint Chiefs shifted in their seats.

One by one, their gaze fell to the chairman, as if waiting for a translation of what the President had just said, for none wanted to contemplate what each thought the President meant.

"General Lancaster," the President asked, "what is the status of the Second Marine Division?"

General Robert Lancaster, Commandant of the Marine Corps, looked across the table at the President. His face was an emotionless mask as he said simply, "They're ready, sir."

"Very good," the President said. "Can anyone here give me a good reason why I shouldn't send the Second Marine Division to Mississippi?"

For what felt to Norman like three hours, no one moved, even though he desperately wanted to scream that the President was acting like a fool. General Peter MacKenzie, Chairman of the Joint Chiefs of Staff, broke the frigid silence.

"Mr. President...perhaps there are other options more, uh, palatable than an armed response," the general said.

"Such as?" the President asked, turning to the general.

"General MacKenzie, if I may?" Norman had regained his composure and jumped into the fray.

"Certainly, Director Norman," General MacKenzie said. Norman could tell that MacKenzie was more than happy to let him take another salvo from the boss.

The President turned quickly to face Norman once again.

"Mr. President," Norman said steadily, "your earlier comment notwithstanding, this is still a criminal matter, at least in the eyes of the ATF, and it's a matter that can still be contained and brought to closure by the ATF. In fact, we are assembling a task force to do that very thing right this minute."

The President did not respond directly to Norman. Instead he queried the Chairman. "General?"

Peter MacKenzie had thirty-four years active-duty service in the U.S. Army, two wars under his belt, more decorations than he could remember, an impressive resume of commands, and a reputation as an intellectual. At this moment, however, he was suddenly aware that none of his previous accomplishments or commands or duty stations could help him answer this question.

"Mr. President, first of all let me say that if the decision is made to send troops into Mississippi for the purpose of conducting combat operations against the Mississippi People's Militia," he said, "I believe that I speak for all of us when I say that you will have our complete and total support."

"But?" the President said.

"But, Mr. President, before that decision is made, all possible options should be considered and analyzed. I believe at this point, Director Norman is the 'go to guy.' He has a man on the ground, his info is already developed and familiar with his agency, and his people are more than capable of handling themselves in a firefight. To send troops in at this point, while certainly proving a point and providing a considerable deterrent demonstration, may not have complete public support."

The President slumped in his chair and considered MacKenzie's advice, which, to Norman, sounded a lot like the most senior general in the United States was very gently telling the Commander in Chief not to go off half-cocked and act like an ass.

"Charles, how long until you can have these guys in jail?" he asked.

Now Norman shifted in his seat. "It depends, sir, on where they are, what they're doing, but we should be able to have them in custody within seventy-two hours, provided they don't leave the country."

"You've got thirty-six," the President said. He turned once again to General MacKenzie. "Peter, in thirty-six hours I want to be briefed on the plan to mobilize the Second Marine Division and all supporting units into the state of Mississippi. At the conclusion of that brief, if the MPM is still at large, the deployment will begin immediately."

MacKenzie simply replied, "Yessir."

The plan the President referred to was the one on Conklin's desk. Support from Air Force recon satellites and F117A "Stealth" fighter aircraft had been added. The Army, much to the displeasure of its service chief, would play only a reserve role. Fort Bragg's 82nd Airborne Division and Fort Stewart's 24th Infantry Division (Mechanized) constituted this reserve.

"That is all, gentlemen," the President said as he left the room. The generals jumped to their feet ahead of the civilians as the President strode out of the Tank. A disbelieving Charles Norman followed the throng into the Pentagon.

What have we done? he thought over and over as he walked to his car in the Pentagon parking lot.

The whole situation had spun out of control. A division of Marines? In Mississippi? Norman wondered if the President had lost his mind. He remembered a line from the oath of office he took twenty-five years earlier when he was commissioned in the Navy. "...against all enemies, foreign and domestic..."

He knew what it meant, but, he thought, this was crazy. The MPM wasn't a domestic enemy. Norman had wanted to scream at the generals during the President's edict—until he saw their faces. He realized then that they too had their misgivings about this operation. Then why hadn't they said something more emphatic than MacKenzie's terse little speech?

Norman cursed the military culture which produced the "Yessir, yessir, three bags full" mentality.

There was only one way to prevent this lunacy, Norman thought as his driver negotiated the traffic on the interstate. Stuart had to stop the militia before the Marines got to Mississippi. But how? The man was running for his life.

Norman lifted the car phone from its cradle and dialed Raymond Carr's number.

Stuart stood in a phone booth just off the south side of the town square in Oxford. He scanned his surroundings, searching intently but finding nothing unusual. He gripped the phone tightly to his ear. Assistant Director Carr had just finished briefing him about the director's meeting with the President.

"It went badly, to say the least," Carr said. "The President screamed for about half an hour, first at Norman when he gave a status report on you, then at the Joint Chiefs when they hesitated at his recommendation to deploy the Second Marine Division immediately."

Stuart thought everyone in Washington, D.C., had gone completely insane. "What next?" he asked.

"Now, you're really running out of time," Carr said. "The President didn't know that I'd given you permission to meet with the Jackson office. That's what got him so mad. I'm not sure we can stop the deployment, but you have to arrest them—at least Moreland. Norman got the President to hold off for thirty-six hours. After that he said he would use all means necessary."

"Was that the phrase the President used?"

"Yes," Carr said.

"Does that apply to me, too?" Stuart asked.

"Special Agent Stuart, you are to arrest him, do you understand?"

A long pause. Stuart gazed through the scratched Plexiglas of the phone booth. "Yeah I understand." He paused. "Have you people lost your minds? Is the President seriously considering sending a division of Marines into this state?"

"He was serious about Posse Comitatus, wasn't he?"

"Does he have any idea how many people are going to get killed?" Stuart said. "Does he realize that the very instant those troops cross the state line, the MPM will most likely triple in size? This is the South, remember. We've had federal troops occupy this state before and the reception then was pretty cold."

"Look, I really don't want to get into an argument with you over the morality, legality and practicality of this," Carr said. "I'm more concerned that you're beginning to sound a little like a militiaman. As a matter of fact, that thought has crossed my mind several times in the last few weeks. It's not unusual for an agent to get too close to his subject, especially when the agent is working as deep as you've been. Wade, I realize you're on your native soil and that you're naturally emotional about issues regarding Mississippi. Are you going to be able to think clearly on this?"

"Are you questioning my loyalty?" Stuart asked.

"Not at all," Carr said. "Nor am I second-guessing you. But you're pretty worked up at the moment."

"You're damn right I am. You tell me that the President is sending in a division of Marines unless I stop an entire militia by myself in thirty-six hours and I'm not supposed to be worked up over that?"

Carr said, "Regardless, we have one last chance to get this right. We'll have a task force in Bedford by tomorrow morning. It will fall under your direct supervision immediately."

"Bedford's no good," Stuart said. "The MPM will know something's up and take off. We need an assembly area."

"Okay, where?"

Stuart thought. "Highway 94, at the west side of the county line. I can meet everyone there. That's closer to the compound than Bedford. Have them meet me at sunup."

"I'll let them know," Carr said. "What are you going to do in the meantime?"

"Try to stay alive."

11

Stuart glanced at his watch. 1651. Twilight seeped through the campus, bringing on a chilly fall night.

He approached Lee Ann's dormitory cautiously. Although he hadn't seen his pursuers or any police in the hours since he left the MPM compound, he sensed they were out there.

He walked downhill from the student union building between two older dorms, quickly crossed the street, and continued downhill to Lee Ann's dormitory. He scanned the parking lot for her car.

When he located it, he moved to a position between two vehicles where he could see both Lee Ann's car and the front entrance to the dorm.

He waited impatiently for five o'clock, which came and went with no sign of Lee Ann. Irritated, he checked his watch again—1705. He ran for the front door of the dorm.

Inside, he asked the woman at the desk, a part-time student worker, if Lee Ann had come down from her room already.

"Sure has, about forty-five minutes ago," she told him. "She met some guy."

Stuart fished his credentials out of his coat pocket and flashed them before the woman's startled face.

"Lee Ann—Miss Weatherby—may be in considerable danger. Do you remember what this man looked like?" he asked.

The girl wrinkled her brow. "His name was Charlie. He was older than you," she said. "Tall, skinny, tanned. I guess Lee Ann knew who he was."

Stuart started. "What makes you say that?"

"Well, when she came off the elevator and saw him standing here, she looked real surprised and said to him, 'Charlie, what are you doing here?'"

Stuart felt a flash of anger.

"Did you see them leave?" he asked.

"I only saw them leave the lobby here," she said.

Stuart tried to remain calm. He thanked the girl and dashed out of the dorm and up the hill leading to the union. He had to get back to his car. And go where?

Stuart's mind raced as he ran across campus in the growing darkness. He tried to guess Tanner's next move.

The only reason for kidnapping Lee Ann was to lure him into a trap, Stuart reasoned. He accepted this and decided on the direct approach—he would take the cheese and leave the mouse trap unsprung. But where was the trap?

As Stuart flung his pack into his car and started the engine, he realized that there was only one place to which Tanner could be expected to lure him, the MPM compound.

Stuart knew that Tanner would have the entrance blocked and would feel secure within the barbed wire and Claymore mines that made up the perimeter.

But what Tanner didn't know—and the thought made Stuart smile—was that when Stuart emplaced the wire and mines, he left gaps that allowed quick access into the compound. Originally, the gaps were intended for the use of an ATF task force, but not now.

He floored the accelerator. As he sped through the black Mississippi night, he recalled the President's words, as relayed by Raymond Carr. He planned to free Lee Ann by all means necessary.

He entered Junkin County on Highway 10 from the east and took back roads to avoid the town of Bedford, just in case Gage or his deputies were prowling. He turned north onto Highway 23 and several minutes later turned west onto U.S. Highway 94. He closed on the secondary road which led to the MPM compound. He roared past it, then pulled to the shoulder and killed the engine. He knew the compound was nearly three miles from the highway, not a difficult walk, even in the thick woods, especially with night vision goggles.

Stuart reached into his pack and grabbed his pistols. He jammed them in the small of his back. He took a quick reading from the cheap luminous compass attached to his watchband and slipped the NVGs over his head. When his eyes had adjusted to the green landscape produced by the glasses, he hiked off.

Forty minutes later, he stepped through one of his gaps in the perimeter wire, on the west side of the compound near an ammunition bunker. He thought about re-orienting some of the Claymores to wreck the bunkers, but quickly discarded the idea, as he was more concerned with finding Lee Ann.

He moved quickly around the north side of the bunker complex, using the inky gloom of the rifle range on his left to his advantage. He covered the few hundred yards to the main compound in seconds, aided by the daylight-like effects of the night vision goggles.

The main compound had floodlights around its perimeter, but none were turned on, causing Stuart to presume the camp was deserted. There had been no one at the vehicle entrance when he had sneaked around the guard shack twenty minutes earlier. Stuart wondered if he had guessed wrong.

He moved in a crouch to the westernmost building, the one which housed Moreland's office. The windows were dark. Stuart heard nothing and crossed the open space to a building on the south side. He detected no signs of life.

At the adjacent building, however, Stuart stopped in midstride as he rounded the corner of the structure. A shaft of yellow light angled out of the window, nearly blinding him as the NVGs amplified the light to a painful level. He had moved so fast that he had seen the light before he had time to take off the goggles.

Stuart cursed silently as he ripped the goggles from his head and let them hang around his neck. He yanked his revolver from his back. He hunkered below the window, straining to hear anything that might be happening inside while his eyes readjusted. He heard the unmistakable twang of Charlie Tanner's voice. Stuart slowly thumbed back the Magnum's hammer. He shut his eyes and mentally oriented himself.

The building was one of the barracks, so called only because military-issue cots had been thrown inside some months back. On occasion, militia members—those from out of town—spent the night in the building's small, cramped interior.

Stuart's head snapped up when he heard Tanner's voice grow louder.

"Oh, he'll be here, all right," Tanner said. "There's no way he's just going to let her disappear without a fight."

Stuart slowly raised himself to peer through the window. He held his breath, hoping that the next sound he heard would not be glass shattering as a bullet struck him in the forehead.

Lee Ann Weatherby was tied to a cot against one wall of the building. Her hands were bound together behind her head and her legs bound on either side of the cot. Her mouth was gagged. Her skirt was bunched around her waist, and her blouse had been ripped. Her bra and panties had been removed. Her eyes flashed hotly, a mixture of terror, contempt and anger.

At the foot of the cot, Tanner and another man Stuart had never seen before leered at Lee Ann.

Stuart dropped below the window to regain his composure. His breath came in short gasps until he fought his anger back under control.

He stood to the side of the window and looked in again. Tanner and the other man were laughing obscenely as Lee Ann thrashed helplessly on the cot. Tanner was facing Stuart as he stood over the girl and for an instant Stuart thought he'd be seen, but quickly realized that, since Tanner was inside a lighted room looking out, he would only be able to see his own reflection.

Tanner began unbuckling his belt, laughing. A strange look settled over his face, a curious cross between sexual desire and something Stuart couldn't define as he aimed his pistol at Tanner's head.

Tanner dropped his pants. Stuart impulsively lowered his pistol and aimed in again, this time on Tanner's exposed crotch. Stuart's mind seemed to detach itself from his body, as it always did in such situations. His senses took control of his body. Tanner's companion turned away from the scene, as if embarrassed.

Stuart squeezed the trigger just as Tanner reached for Lee Ann. The big Magnum roared as the 158-grain hollow-point bullet smashed through the glass, sending slivers of glass flying in all directions. Stuart felt as if the scene was happening in slow motion. It was almost as if he could actually see the bullet spinning toward Charlie Tanner.

The bullet hit Tanner squarely in the groin. Tanner, looking down when Stuart fired, staggered backward as his genitals exploded in a red cloud. Tanner screamed, a high-pitched animal howl that Stuart knew he would never forget, even as he pivoted to aim at Tanner's companion.

Tanner grabbed his groin and sank to his knees, retching and vomiting as blood gushed from his midsection.

Stuart fired again, this time at the other man, who had recovered from his initial shock and wheeled away toward an M16 leaning against the wall opposite Stuart. The bullet struck him behind the right ear, completely blowing out his forehead and most of his face and spewing brain and tissue onto the wall. He collapsed in a heap against the wall.

Stuart vaulted through the wrecked window. He walked calmly toward Tanner, who had drawn himself into the fetal position. He lay in an enormous pool of blood and vomit, whimpering like a wounded animal. Stuart stood over him. Tanner glared back. Stuart leveled his pistol at Tanner's head and watched Tanner's facial expression change from defiance to the realization that death was near. Stuart fired, hitting Tanner squarely in the forehead and killing him instantly.

Stuart shoved his weapon into his jeans and turned to Lee Ann. He felt as if hours had passed since he fired his first round, even though he had killed both men in less than a minute.

Stuart snatched a pocketknife from his hip pocket and cut Lee Ann free. She bounded from the cot, snatching the gag from her mouth. She flung her arms around him.

"Oh my God, Wade, oh my God," she said in a trembling voice over and over again.

Stuart held her tightly for as long as he dared as he waited for the shakes to come. When he felt his hands begin to tremble, he released her. "We gotta get moving," he said.

Stuart snatched up the rifle and handed it to Lee Ann, who took the weapon without protest. He crawled through the window and helped Lee Ann down to the ground. He took Lee Ann by the hand and led her out of the compound.

As they crashed through the darkness, Stuart was thankful that Lee Ann kept up step for step. He shut his mind to the scene of death he'd just left, compartmentalizing the emotions for a time when he could better deal with them, along with all the others he had on hold, waiting to haunt him.

They came to Stuart's car and scrambled inside. Stuart fired up the engine and shot onto the highway in a luminous cloud of silver dust and gravel.

"Where are we going?" Lee Ann finally asked five minutes later.

"I don't know," Stuart said, more sharply than he intended. He softened his tone. "Are you okay? Did they—"

"No," Lee Ann said. "I guess they didn't have time before you...shot them. I'm sorry I ever doubted you."

"Forget it. I didn't expect you to accept a story as unbelievable as this one on its face. I'm just sorry that I let you out of my sight."

"Not as sorry as Charlie Tanner," Lee Ann said.

Stuart glanced at her, somewhat startled by her comment. Her eyes glittered back at him.

"No, I guess not," he said.

Stuart checked his watch—0107. A little more than twenty-four hours left until the President ordered in the Marines. And now he had to get Lee Ann to a safe house, or at least a safe motel room. Stuart wondered how long it would take Gage or Moreland to discover the corpses of Charlie Tanner and his companion. He wondered idly what their reactions would be to seeing Tanner with his dick shot off.

"So now what?" Lee Ann asked.

"I need to get you somewhere safe, then I have to go back to Bedford," Stuart said.

"Back to Bedford? Are you crazy?"

"Orders. I've got to arrest your uncle—or at least make it possible for an ATF task force to do so—or the President is going to order the Second Marine Division into Mississippi to destroy the MPM."

"What?" Lee Ann asked.

Stuart nodded. "My reaction was a little stronger than that."

"But why on earth would the President want to do that?"

"Well," Stuart began as he decided to drive to Tunica, in the Delta, to leave Lee Ann at a casino hotel, "if you listen to your uncle and some of his contemporaries, it's just the proof that the federal government has been creeping into our lives for years, slowly eroding our personal freedoms and setting us up for a military takeover."

"That's insane. Why would our president try to use his own military to take over his own country? This isn't Central America."

Stuart smiled. He had already asked himself the same question.

"The current theory among the right-wingers is that it's not our country anymore," Stuart said. "The military takes orders. Our military takes orders from civilians—politicians who make policy and in some cases order the military to enforce it. The President has declared the MPM a threat to the national security and the militia members enemies of the nation. So the military has been ordered to confront an enemy. It makes no difference that the enemy is American and is on American soil...at least that's the theory. The military's reason for being is to defend the Constitution—against all enemies, foreign and domestic."

Stuart peered through the windshield at a road sign, then wheeled the car through a left turn onto Highway 4. He headed west toward the vast flatness of the Mississippi Delta.

"I'm taking you to a casino hotel," he said to Lee Ann.

"How romantic."

Stuart said, "Just stay there—in the room—for a few days, until all this is taken care of. Don't come out of that room unless it's on fire. Order room service."

"I'm not staying in a room for days," Lee Ann said. "You might as well turn around right now because I'm staying with you."

"Lee Ann," Stuart said sharply enough to make her flinch. "You saw what happened to two men about an hour ago. More of that is likely to happen. You're going to a hotel room and that's all there is to it."

Lee Ann slumped back against the car seat.

Stuart topped a final hill then descended into the expanse of the Delta, the prehistoric bottom of the Mississippi River. He had always been amazed at the suddenness with which the Delta appeared and how it completely overwhelmed his senses with its enormity. His feeling of being overwhelmed was much more acute at the moment, in the early morning darkness, when the black velvet, punctured only occasionally by an electric light, engulfed him like a cool, wet organism battling him for the very air in his lungs. Because he had not grown up here, Stuart could never get used to the Delta.

Stuart squinted into the darkness ahead, read a sign and veered hard to the right onto a side road, causing Lee Ann to draw in her breath.

Stuart knew that five years ago the road had not existed. The casinos changed that.

With the legalization of riverboat gambling, family tradition was tossed away like yesterday's paper. Land which had been in Mississippi families for almost two hundred years—cotton land—was sold overnight in get-rich-quick schemes. A strip of land such as the one Stuart now drove through offered prime, quick access to the burgeoning casino strip in Tunica. Casino owners would pay any price for the access and shrewd Mississippi plantation owners were happy to charge any price. The result was richer casino owners, richer plantation owners, but not much change for the people of Tunica County, one of the poorest in the nation, with most of the population on food stamps.

He tore down the two-lane blacktop road that knifed through a cotton field, bathed in the harsh orange glow of street lights. He passed quickly through the crumbling downtown area of Tunica, home to the infamous "Sugar Ditch," a festering pustule of raw sewage that meandered through the black neighborhoods.

He slowed the car as he approached the obscenity of the neon that screamed at him and invaded his car. Had he noticed, he would have seen Lee Ann squinting in the hard light, an unpleasant look on her pretty face.

He steered into the parking lot of one of the newer casinos, Circus Circus, and threw the car into parking gear. He looked over at Lee Ann, who wore a look of disgust.

"I'm going inside," Stuart said. "I'll get you a room and then I'll take you in."

"You're crazy," Lee Ann said.

Stuart sighed. He admired, respected and even loved Lee Ann, but now was not the time to argue.

"Lee Ann," he said, "I don't have time to argue with you. If I have to, I'll carry you into a room and lock you in myself."

Lee Ann stared at him for a long moment, then shrugged. "Okay, Wade," she said.

Twenty minutes later, Stuart breathed easily as he hurtled down Highway 4 out of the Delta. His head hurt and he was very tired, but he relaxed somewhat, knowing Lee Ann was safe.

He checked his watch as he passed a sign informing him that he had just entered the corporation limits of Senatobia. He had about twenty hours left.

He turned left at a three-way stop, then right at another and headed through downtown Senatobia, a tiny, sleepy town nestled against a railroad line and Interstate 55.

A one-traffic-light town, Senatobia's only claims to fame were that Yankees burned the town during the Civil War and Confederate General Nathan Bedford Forrest used the town as a staging area for his raids on Memphis. Beyond those events, the most important recent news was that a Senatobia boy had played quarterback at Ole Miss a couple of years earlier.

Stuart crossed the railroad tracks, built on a fill similar to a levee. The town had only barely begun to come to life as he passed the Peoples Bank, then a fast-food restaurant on his way to the intersection of Highway 4 and Interstate 55. When he stopped at the traffic light he noticed the "4-55 Truck Stop" to his left. Stuart wheeled in, yawning as he pulled into a parking space.

Ten minutes later, as he walked out the truck stop with a large Styrofoam cup of coffee, Stuart felt somewhat more refreshed. He was exhausted to the point of being mentally dull, and he knew it. Things would have to wait until he could get a few hours rest. He impulsively decided to get a room at the motel across the street, to hell with the Washington Warriors.

And then he saw Sheriff Tom Gage.

The sheriff stood next to his official car, talking to a local who shook his head several times, as if he could not answer several questions asked by the lawman.

Stuart froze. Gage was directly between him and his car.

Stuart decided to get back inside the truck stop and look for a rear exit. But, at the instant he moved, Gage seemed to decide to go into the building as well. He turned and was face to face with Stuart, separated only by about fifteen yards of asphalt.

Stuart crouched and noticed Gage's right hand already moving toward his revolver. Stuart dropped the coffee without even realizing it and yanked at the .45 in the small of his back.

Although younger, Stuart wasn't much faster than Gage. He leveled his pistol and fired at Gage even as the sheriff pulled his trigger.

Stuart heard no sounds. He felt the automatic pistol buck four times in his hands. He saw his muzzle flashes and one from Tom Gage's pistol. He felt a hot blast of air very close to the left side of his face.

He sensed that his body was moving, toward the ground and to his right, lowering his center of gravity as he moved toward cover. He saw Gage's big frame jerk upright, shiver, then reel backward in a pink haze.

Stuart's first bullet hit Gage high in the center of the chest, slamming him up. The second and third bullets hit lower, near the solar plexus, driving him backward, barely alive.

The final bullet hit Gage in the face, just under his nose. It traveled through his sinus cavity, transferring all its hydrostatic energy to the inside of Gage's cranium. Hardly slowed, the projectile plowed through his brain and exploded out the back of his head, near the crown.

The sheriff's head burst open in a misty pink cloud an instant before his body crashed to the asphalt with a wet thump.

Stuart dove behind a car, rolled on his right shoulder and sprang back to his feet. As soon as he saw the crumpled body of Gage, he forced his muscles to relax. His eyes scanned the parking lot.

The man Gage had questioned stood, transfixed and trembling, behind the sheriff's car. Stuart glared at him and waved his pistol at the man, a signal to leave.

The motion broke the man's trance and he ran away.

Stuart, not waiting for a dozen witnesses to appear, sprinted to his car, dove in and hit the ignition. Within seconds, he hurtled up the northbound ramp of I-55, toward Memphis.

12

Washington, specifically, the President of the United States and, consequently, the director of the Bureau of Alcohol, Tobacco and Firearms, did not take the news of the death of Sheriff Thomas Gage well.

The President became apoplectic upon receiving the report from the director that Stuart had shot and killed Gage. The President's face turned dark an instant before he exploded in anger at Norman.

"Goddamnit!" the President screamed, the profanity echoing obscenely off the walls of the Oval Office. He pointed a finger menacingly at Norman and jabbed the air between them.

"Your agent is totally out of control," the President said. "You told me ATF was capable of handling this. So far, the ATF's way of handling this situation is to kill three people—I mean shot them full of holes— while doing nothing to bring this organization to heel."

The President, in a characteristic calm-down, slumped back in the large leather chair behind his desk. He looked at Norman, his eyes flat and hard. Norman felt as if he were a teenager again, being chastised by his father.

"Charles," the President said. "You realize that I don't really have a choice now."

Bullshit, Norman thought. You've got plenty of choices. You're the President of the United States. You're doing this because you choose to.

The President looked at Norman. "You disagree, Charles?"

"Mr. President," Norman said, wondering if what he were about to say would end his career as a civil servant. Suddenly he decided he didn't care. "This is a law enforcement matter, not a military one. The repeal of Posse Comitatus notwithstanding, there is no foundation whatsoever for sending federal troops to Mississippi. This isn't the '60s and this isn't some campus disturbance. These troops will combat-deploy just the same as if they were overseas. But they won't be deploying against a foreign enemy. These Marines, our nation's armed forces, are going to be facing other Americans. Do you realize what that means, Mr. President?"

The President looked irritated. "Yes, Charles, I do. Just as, I'm sure, Abraham Lincoln did when he ordered the U.S. Army into action against the Confederacy."

Now Norman grew irritated. "It's not the same, goddamnit," he said crossly, knowing he was as good as fired. "That was an open act of sedition and aggression. This is a small radical group that needs to be chased down and arrested!"

The President stared at the ATF director. "Charles," he said, "frankly, the ATF's efforts to bring this 'small radical group' to heel have been found wanting."

He stood behind his desk and gazed out the window. He removed his glasses and clasped his hands behind his back, apparently lost in thought.

"I've never served in the military," the President said in a detached way. "You did, and I'm not going to presume that I know what it's like to be a member of the military. But I have read the Constitution. And I have read, many times, the oath of office a military officer swears to—and I'm sure that surprises you."

He glanced at Norman, who remained expressionless. "I know what the oath says," he continued. "It says, 'I swear to support and defend the Constitution of the United States against all enemies, foreign and domestic.'"

The President turned from the Oval Office window and looked at Norman.

"Foreign and domestic, Charles. Do you see why I have no choice?"

"Mr. President," Norman protested, his voice imploring. "These guys are less a domestic enemy than they are firearm violators. And you're right, sir. You never served in the military."

The President shot a look at Norman.

The director, considering his imminent firing a foregone conclusion, decided to go full throttle. "Our servicemen are a unique bunch," he said. "They're all patriotic, as far as I'm concerned. But what really makes them unique, far different from any other army, is they demand to know why they are being sent to fight. And rightly so. They are going to ask why. What is the answer going to be? That the Mississippi People's Militia is a threat to the national security? They won't buy it, Mr. President."

The President sighed, exasperated. "Charles, who determines domestic policy in this country?"

"You do, Mr. President."

"And who is commander-in-chief of the military?"

"You are, Mr. President."

"Thank you, Charles. You may go now."

Charles Norman exhaled abruptly, as if he had been gut-punched. Stiffly, he reached to his belt and removed the badge he had worn for thirty-three years.

Without a word, he jammed the badge onto the President's desk. Tears welled in his eyes. He spun on his heels and left the Oval Office, knowing he would never see it again.

As the door closed silently, the President glanced sideways at the director's badge. He picked it up and fingered the lettering absently.

Is this how Lincoln felt? Always looking for leaders, taking the high ground when nobody believed in him? He stared at the iron fence across the White House lawn. *No wonder Lincoln aged so rapidly.*

He turned from the window and sank heavily into his chair. He leaned to his right and punched a button on his telephone.

"SECDEF," he said.

The Secretary of Defense came on the line twelve seconds later. "Yessir," he said.

"Do it. Commence Operation Home Guard," the President said. A long pause. "Very well, sir," the SECDEF replied.

In North Carolina, Major General Conklin held his head in his hands. Even though he had prepared himself and had tried to convince himself that this was simply another deployment, he felt overwhelmed with his own disbelief.

His conversation with the Commandant, which ended only minutes before, had been brief. Conklin felt as if the Commandant was being intentionally terse, for fear that one, or both of them, might say what he actually felt. Conklin sighed and lifted himself out of his chair. He could drive himself crazy arguing both sides of this one. He had made his own decision.

I serve my country, he thought. He had been given a lawful order by the Commandant of the Marine Corps and, once removed, the President of the United States. It did not matter what he felt of the order, if he did not like it. He had followed orders he did not like many times before.

His job, as commanding general of the Second Marine Division, was to deploy his troops in accordance with the orders of the President, and he would do it to the utmost of his ability.

He walked out of his office and across the hall to his chief of staff's office to begin the deployment.

Three hours later, Stuart punched Carr's number on a pay phone in the lobby of the Peabody Hotel in downtown Memphis. The lobby was jammed with tourists and the business crowd, who gathered around the elegant hotel's water fountain as they awaited the peculiar daily parade of ducks from a rooftop coop through the lobby to the water. Stuart wanted the crowd. At the moment, he felt a room full of witnesses would do him more good than harm.

Carr was angry when he came on the line. "Damn it, Wade, you're not making this any easier, are you?" he said.

"I'm doing fine, thanks," Stuart said. "I take it you heard that I had to kill Gage."

Carr sighed. "Yes, it was just on the news. And the President saw it, too. The director just came from there. The President said you were totally out of control, embarrassed Norman in front of a room full of senior military officers, and said the ATF way of conducting an investigation has produced three, maybe four dead bodies so far."

Stuart's anger rose. "Did anybody bother to tell him that if there weren't four dead bodies right now, I'd be dead?" he said. "Did Norman even try to tell the President that his plan is insane?"

"Yes he did," Carr said. "After the generals left the Oval Office an hour ago, Norman said he had a personal audience with the President. He went to bat for you, Wade, and he stood up for what he believed in, which is that sending a division of troops into Mississippi is illegal, immoral and can only result in God knows how many deaths. He stood right there in front of the President's desk and told off the leader of the most powerful country in the world, then he took his badge off and left it on his desk."

Stuart felt like he had been kicked in the stomach. "I'm sorry," he said.

"Just thought you'd like to know. He had thirty-three years in."

"This is fucking crazy," Stuart said as he watched the Peabody ducks waddle into the fountain. "What happens now?"

Carr explained that, after Norman left the White House, the President ordered the Secretary of Defense to commence Operation Home Guard, as the deployment of the Second Marine Division had been named.

Stuart shook his head as he listened to Carr. When the assistant director was done, Stuart hung up the phone.

Did the President really know what he was doing? No, he never spent a single day in uniform, a uniform Stuart wore for ten years. He never had to deal with the fear of combat. He never put a kid in a bag or stepped on a Marine's brain while trying to find what was left of him after a fucking rocket attack.

Stuart fumed as he thought about the Marines in North Carolina, who were already packing their gear.

Americans join the military for many different reasons, he told himself. To save money for college; to see the world; to get away from Mom and Dad; or because Dad was in the service, which was particularly true in the Marine Corps.

But Americans, many of them, joined out of pure patriotism— a belief in the nation, freedom and the Constitution. The patriotism, Stuart knew, was not blind loyalty, and he did not expect a single Marine in the Second Division to risk his life without knowing why.

Marines would fight to the death for something they believed in, even if no one else in the country would, Stuart thought. But they had to know why, and the why better be clearly stated and worth dying for.

But, Stuart knew, Marines also fought for another reason: for each other. Stuart knew the bond created between men in battle. It was a bond of trust and love that no one could understand unless it was experienced firsthand. It was a love every bit as intense, and every bit as different, as that between a husband and wife. And it was a bond that transcended race or creed, or what part of the country you were from. It didn't matter. You were Americans suffering together and drawing strength from that and from the knowledge that what you were fighting for had a purpose—a just purpose. He had lost his youth on the sands of the Arabian desert to learn that lesson.

A lesson the President never learned. Now, he's ordering the nation's armed forces to gun down its own citizens and expects the military to call that a just mission, Stuart thought bitterly.

He recalled the California survey again, and finally remembered the results. The overwhelming majority—something on the order of eighty to eighty-five percent—stated strongly that they would never raise their weapons at fellow Americans.

Eighty-five percent, Stuart thought. Potential mutiny? He knew better. And he knew Marines. In that unique and contradictory way of Marines, he knew that same eighty-five percent would also say that they would follow the orders of the officers appointed above them, both civilian and military, and that they would follow the orders of their commander in chief.

I do solemnly swear to support and defend the Constitution of the United States against all enemies, foreign and domestic, Stuart recited in his head. That I will bear true faith and allegiance to the same.

Stuart knew the oath by heart. He had taken it each time he had been promoted—three times—and had administered it countless times to Marines he had promoted or re-enlisted. He had taken every word seriously.

Would the Marines fight? In the end, Stuart reasoned, they would, if the President was convincing that this militia was in fact a domestic enemy—and if the American public supported it.

But how could Americans support it? It was ludicrous to think that Americans would welcome armed troops in their neighborhoods.

To Stuart, it all came down to individual conscience. He knew the Marines would each decide according to his or her own conscience, beliefs and loyalty to one another. As would the American public. Sides would be chosen and lives undoubtedly lost, but every American would have to follow his or her conscience.

And my job is to make sure it doesn't get that far, he thought.

"Bullshit."

It wasn't the obscenity itself as much as it was the ferocity with which it bounced off the cinderblock wall of a room in the bachelor officers' quarters.

Inside the room, two infantry lieutenants stared at a third, who had uttered the profanity.

1st Lt. Franklin Belmont, an infantry company executive officer in 2nd Battalion, 8th Marine Regiment, had been in the Marine Corps for nearly three years. He was aggressive and outspoken. He was also the product of the mean streets of Los Angeles, growing up and surviving the gang-ridden South Central section of the city.

He stared at his companions, 1st Lt Jason Wheatley, also an XO in another company, and 2nd Lt. Jack Moretti, a fresh-faced boot from Philadelphia.

Belmont shook his head. "You motherfuckers got to be kidding," he said. He had just heard Wheatley's opinion of their impending deployment to Mississippi. Wheatley had held that deploying federal troops was unconstitutional, a violation of the Bill of Rights, that this was a law-enforcement matter.

"The only reason anybody is pissed off about us going in there and kicking somebody's ass is because these assholes are white," Belmont said. He said the words calmly, almost softly. "Nobody would say shit if we deployed to Compton to bust a few caps at the Crips. That would be okay, because we'd be doing something about the gang problem. What's the difference between the gangs and this militia, huh?"

Wheatley started to say something but snapped his mouth shut. Moretti stared dumbly at the carpet in the BOQ room.

Belmont turned to his half-filled seabag and began stuffing his clothing inside.

"I'll tell you the difference," he said. "They're white and they ain't armed as heavily. That's all. Other than that, they're the same. All they want to do is hate and kill—and teach everybody else to do the same thing. So do I think this is unconstitutional? I don't give a fuck. If the President of the United States wants these motherfuckers dead, that's fine with me. Let's get it on."

That night, Stuart awoke in a motel near Interstate 55 in south

Memphis. He glanced at his watch, then tuned the television to CNN.

A silver-haired man stood bundled up in the darkness on-screen. The bar at the bottom of the screen told Stuart that the reporter's name was James Honeycutt and that he was reporting from Columbus Air Force Base in northeast Mississippi, about a four-hour drive from Memphis and Stuart's motel.

The reporter explained that the deployment of the Second Marine Division had begun hours earlier.

The camera panned back to show a short black man standing beside Honeycutt. The caption changed to read, "Benny Edwards, Local Resident." Honeycutt asked Benny to explain what he had seen.

"I can sleep through anything," Benny said. He pointed at a small silver mobile home. "My trailer is at the end of the runway. Every day, I hear them jets training the pilots, so I don't think nothing about it. But, when I saw on the news that the Marines would probably be coming here, and then I heard the planes tonight, I knew that was them."

Once again, the media shows up—possibly threatening the lives of the Marines involved, Stuart thought as he watched the news.

A live shot was bringing the entire landing—taking place only a few hundred yards away from Honeycutt and Edwards—into Stuart's motel room. He watched with great interest as the plane disgorged overloaded Marines, who ran unsteadily, bent double from the huge packs on their backs, to form a perimeter. The reporter, jabbering incessantly to fill up dead air on the live shot, rattled off some information, most of which Stuart already knew: these Marines were the first elements of the Second Marine; they flew in aboard C-141 cargo planes; there were over a hundred troops on the ground with more on the way; the media was being kept at arm's length.

Stuart continued to watch, shaking his head. This was happening less than two hundred miles from where he sat. But he felt as if he were watching a U.S. invasion of a foreign country. What happens next? Armed guards at checkpoints all over the state? The phrase "occupied territory" jumped into his mind and made him angry. He flung the remote control against the wall and swore.

13

Stuart stared through his night vision goggles at Amos Moreland's second-story bedroom window and swore to himself.

He was cold, even with his jacket. There would be a frost tonight—or this morning, Stuart reminded himself as he squatted against a pine tree. He held the NVGs to his eyes.

His immediate problem was finding Moreland. Stuart had seen no trace of him in the last few hours he had spent combing the county. Stuart only hoped that he had not taken off for Jackson to finish the task of killing the governor.

An ATF task force was in the air, Stuart had been told two hours earlier. With any luck at all, that team would be making arrests at the MPM compound by midmorning, Stuart thought. But if he couldn't locate Moreland, there might not be anybody to arrest.

Just before sunrise, Stuart stomped through the cold, damp woods to his car, severely disappointed and irritated.

He started the engine and turned on the heater. As he waited for the car to warm up, he listened to a news report on the radio.

The deployment of the Second Marine Division was well ahead of schedule, the newsman said. In fact, it had turned into an administrative landing for the most part. No shots had been fired in Columbus or Memphis, and the Marines were able to establish perimeters and unload gear without interruption.

Curious onlookers had gathered in Memphis to watch the

Marines, but had been turned away at the front gate to Naval Air Station Millington, Tennessee.

Stuart sat slumped back in the driver's seat, his head resting on the seat.

His eyes snapped open when the radio news reporter began to report on public reaction to the deployment.

"At this point, the reaction is guarded at best," the reporter said. "Most area residents are steadfastly opposed to the militias and are genuinely afraid of the growing violence. But many residents don't necessarily feel that the U.S. military's arrival is the right way to eliminate that threat, and most appear to be taking a 'wait and see' attitude."

Stuart stared out the windshield. The public reaction was more encouraging than he had expected.

But then again, he thought, people weren't dying yet.

He put the car in gear and grabbed his cellular phone from under the seat. As he headed toward the MPM compound, he placed a call to Carr. With the deployment progressing so well, Stuart had even less time.

He updated Carr when the assistant director came on the line and expressed his anger at not being able to locate Moreland.

"Keep looking," Carr said. "The task force will be there in a few hours, and the Marines are already forming up to send a mobile patrol your way."

"Boy, the President's not wasting any time, is he?" Stuart said.

"At this point, I don't care, as long as it ends before somebody else gets killed. If you find Moreland, sit tight and keep him under surveillance. Call me and I'll send the task force to you."

To hell with that, Stuart thought. "Okay. Let's just hope I find him soon."

The lead elements of the Second Marine Division established perimeters at Columbus and the airstrip at Naval Air Station Millington in Memphis to allow for follow-on planeloads of equipment and troops. The grunts shivered in the early morning air as massive C-5A Galaxy cargo planes landed behind them and discharged humvees, 5-ton trucks, ammunition and M198 155mm howitzers.

In Columbus, a low fog rose from the surrounding swamps, giving the unloading an otherworldly feel. There was a greater sense of urgency here, as Columbus had been designated a more vulnerable landing site than Memphis.

Many Marines there had visions of shotgun-toting rednecks greeting their plane, but that had not been the case. Only an eerie, damp silence greeted them. Rather than calm them, however, it made most even more nervous.

Within two hours, 6th Marine Regiment was on the ground, in place and waiting for orders to move out.

That order was issued at 0630 by the regimental commander, Col. John "Boxer" Sullivan. The infantrymen mounted up in 5-ton trucks—amphibious tractors and tanks would be arriving later via "low-boy" trailers—to follow the Light Armored Vehicles of a company from 2nd Light Armored Reconnaissance Battalion.

Sixth Marines' mission was simple—head northwest to link up with 2nd Marines moving south from Memphis in a movement to contact, destroying any armed resistance along the way.

The mission had one caveat: use the minimum force possible. Rumor had it the order came straight from the President. Many officers thought the restriction fatuous and useless. The commanders were left to determine the "minimum force" necessary.

The lead vehicle of the convoy, an LAV-25 with six infantry troops inside, rolled through the Air Force base main gate at 0657, and, for the first time since Reconstruction, federal troops again occupied the Deep South. As the convoy rumbled down Mississippi Highway 50 toward West Point, several Marines realized this; many more wondered if—or when—they would be ambushed.

The commander of the LAV, an infantry staff sergeant named

Singletary, was tired, bored and cramped. The convoy had been on the road for nearly an hour, heading north on U.S. Highway 45 Alternate, a straight stretch of flat asphalt between West Point and Okolona.

A boring stretch, thought the staff sergeant. On either side of the highway were fields, fallow and muddy in the fall wet season. The fields gave way to a clump of bare trees just south of Okolona, on the east side of the road.

Singletary was perched low in the commander's hatch, fighting off the stinging cold air. He never saw the missile that arched out of the treeline and slammed into the front right quarter of his vehicle.

He heard the impact of the round fired from a Light Anti-Armor Weapon, a shaped-charge projectile designed to penetrate armor much thicker than the aluminum covering the LAV. He felt his vehicle shudder under an explosion, but his brain had not yet registered that he was under attack.

The concussion of the explosion smacked into him at the same time the vehicle lurched to a halt on the highway, throwing him violently forward.

"God, we've been blown up!" he thought as he slammed into the steel rim of the cupola. He screamed at the driver through his helmet's intercom boom mike, but got no answer. He ducked inside and smelled and saw smoke filling the interior of the vehicle.

He looked into the driver's compartment and saw the lifeless form of the driver slumped in his seat. Across his back was a deep, slick scarlet gash.

Horrified and angry, Singletary wheeled to face the passenger compartment filled with combat-loaded Marines. The ones that were still alive were spilling out the back hatch. He climbed over two dead Marines and past a third who had only half his face remaining. He clambered out of the vehicle, heard machine gun fire and went down immediately in a ditch by the highway.

The grunts in his vehicle were already returning fire, and he realized that the machine gun fire he heard was incoming, not outgoing.

As soon as the first vehicle exploded, the next vehicle lurched off the road, to be followed by the remainder of the column. The LAV drivers gunned their engines and careened off the road to the right, toward the origin of the missile.

The vehicles were slowed by the soft, sticky mud, but not stopped altogether. Three vehicles fired an ear-splitting burst from the 25mm "Bushmaster" cannon atop each vehicle.

Marines in the trucks behind the LAVs streamed into the ditch that ran parallel to the highway shoulder and the treeline from which the fire came. Their platoon commander and NCOs shouted orders up and down the line as the group maneuvered up to the LAV platoon.

The volume of fire from the treeline increased momentarily when an M60 machine gun raked the lip of the ditch in which the Marines crouched. Bullets from rifles whistled over the Marines' heads as well.

Two LAVs churned through the mud, which seemed like a pot of glue to the drivers, until they were roughly on the flanks of the Marine position. The gunners in each vehicle then began methodically returning fire as the drivers moved their vehicles toward the treeline.

The tactic worked. All fire from the unseen ambushers ceased immediately, prompting the dismounted Marines to peek out of their position.

Realizing the silence, platoon commanders barked orders to NCOs, and Marines poured out of the ditch like boiling water.

Expertly aligning themselves in an assault line, they swept through the treeline, stomping through the thick mud in a crouch.

Silence greeted them in the trees. Whoever had firing at them had vanished. Or at least those still living had vanished. In the treeline lay the corpses of three men in civilian clothes. All appeared to be unarmed, but the Marines correctly deduced that whoever had been with them took their weapons before leaving.

The dead men bore gruesome wounds from the 25mm chain gun; one man had been cut almost in half. Several Marines gawked at the bodies before walking back to the highway to collect their own dead.

Four Marines had been killed. Another six had been wounded, either when the LAV had been hit or from gunfire. The company commander, an angry-looking young captain, spoke tersely into a radio handset, guiding a medical evacuation helicopter. He had lost a little less than ten percent of his company in one firefight.

Noncommissioned officers hustled the Marines into a perimeter in preparation for the helo and set up flares to identify the landing zone in the muddy field next to the highway.

The young Marines, many in their teens, couldn't help but notice the four ponchos on the highway, lying side by side, each with a pair of boots protruding from underneath.

14

S tuart checked his watch for the fifth time that hour. He was out of breath after practically sprinting nearly three miles through the woods surrounding the MPM compound. He approached the main camp area via the rifle range, through the gaps in the perimeter.

Stuart figured he had half an hour before the task force arrived at the rendezvous point. A reasonable man would wait, Stuart thought. But at the moment, he didn't feel too reasonable, and he didn't care what Carr said.

Stuart thought another ATF raid, splashed all over the TV screens, would be the galvanizing event for the militias and all the right-wingers, if the arrival of federal troops had not already been. The far right did not need another martyr.

Or, Stuart corrected himself, the country didn't need another right-wing martyr.

Stuart shuddered as his mind's eye recalled images from Waco, Texas, another ATF op that had ended in disaster. He was acutely aware of how easily this situation could end the same way.

Stuart moved the length of the range in a crouch, just out of sight in the bordering treeline.

His feet moved expertly along the forest floor, making little noise. His eyes roved the area, attuned to the folds and bumps of earth, the shadows and hiding places.

Still in the treeline, he reached the main compound's west side, two buildings away from Moreland's field office. He darted from the trees past the first building.

When he reached the door of the building housing Moreland's office, Stuart thumbcocked the pistol with his right hand as he reached across his body for the doorknob with his left hand. He opened the door and entered the building, pistol at the ready.

The room was empty, except for furniture. Stuart sighed disgustedly and lowered his weapon.

He heard something.

Stuart cocked his head. He thought he was either hallucinating or going crazy.

There it was again, he thought. The very faint sound of voices or a radio transmission. Stuart walked toward Moreland's desk, his ears straining. When he looked behind the desk, his eyes fixed upon a small square of plywood under the rollers of Moreland's chair. He walked around the desk, moved the chair and lifted one corner of the plywood.

Stuart smiled as he looked at a small square trap door in the floor. Quietly, he moved the plywood to one side, then flipped off the pistol's safety.

He grabbed a small handle in a recess in the door and deftly yanked it open with his left hand.

He heard his heart pounding as he aimed his pistol down a dimly lighted wooden ladder. The intermittent sound of radio transmissions could be heard coming from what appeared to be an underground chamber off to the side at the bottom of the ladder, about eight feet below.

Stuart started to climb down the ladder, then changed his mind. He positioned himself so that he would be facing the dim light at the bottom of the ladder, and stepped into the pit.

He dropped and landed squarely on his feet. In a squatting position, he snapped his pistol up to eye level, aimed at the head of a very startled Amos Moreland.

Moreland dropped the AN/PRC-77 military radio handset onto the military-issue field desk in front of him as Stuart stood quickly, his aim never wavering. Moreland slowly placed both hands on the desk.

"Hello, Wade," he said flatly.

"Don't even blink or I'll kill you," Stuart said.

"Like you killed Tom Gage?"

"Exactly."

Stuart chanced a look around. Plywood walls and floor, field desk, battered lamp. Behind Moreland sat the radio. In the corner to Stuart's right was a small table with a color television and VCR. The television was on, with the volume low. Moreland, who had not moved, stared impassively at Stuart.

"Now," Stuart said slowly, "You're going to tell me who's supposed to be doing the governor."

Moreland laughed bitterly as he stared down the barrel of Stuart's pistol. "Well now, Wade, you already figured that one out, it seems. Those plans got put on hold when you killed Charlie Tanner."

Stuart didn't know whether to believe Moreland. The old man's eyes narrowed.

"That plan ended when you murdered Charlie," Moreland said.

"Murdered?" Stuart shot back. "Was kidnapping and rape part of your plan?" Stuart noticed the confusion on Moreland's face.

"Did you plan on having Tanner kidnap your niece, tie her up and rape her like an animal?"

Moreland pointed a trembling finger at Stuart and attempted to speak.

Stuart cut him off. "Shut the fuck up. Your days as militia commander are over."

Moreland grinned. "Not quite. I've been getting reports from the ambush site," he said matter-of-factly. He smirked when he saw surprise appear on Stuart's face. "Just south of Okolona. Marine convoy heading north—toward us, I suppose. Killed a few."

Stuart felt the anger rise in his throat, but fought it down. "How many?"

"Looks like about half a dozen." Moreland jerked his head

toward the television. "It'll be back on the news any minute now. The Marines are even holding a press conference. Go on, turn it up and watch it yourself."

Stuart held the gun steady on the old man. "Turn it up," he said, nodding toward the television.

Moreland obeyed Stuart then sat in his chair. Stuart positioned himself so that he was able to aim his pistol at Moreland's head while he watched the screen.

A commercial ended and the picture of Marine Colonel Mike Busch in front of a map of Mississippi appeared. The news report had cut in late, and the colonel had already begun his brief. Stuart recognized the symbols on the map that indicated the route of the convoy as he listened to Busch reconstruct the events that led up to the ambush.

As he listened to Busch describe the fight, Stuart's anger rose. He contemplated squeezing his trigger. He fought his rage down and concentrated on the colonel's words.

"How many civilians were killed?" a reporter blurted out.

Busch glared at him. "The Marines found in the treeline the bodies of three militiamen in civilian clothes. There could have been more wounded, but we don't know that at this point."

"How many Marines are dead, colonel?" an elderly reporter asked.

"Four," Busch said. He sighed. "Another six were wounded, either when the LAV was hit or from gunfire."

The picture cut abruptly to a studio where a grim-looking man announced that he had a live report from Sandy Johnson, who was at the scene. The picture changed to a very pretty blonde reporter, whose name appeared in a caption at the bottom of the screen. She stood next to a Marine she introduced as Captain Hernandez, the company commander. He ignored Miss Johnson as he spoke into a radio handset.

"The mood here is understandably hostile," Johnson said. "I've been here about half an hour, and most of these young Marines have never seen combat. They're very angry about the loss of their comrades in arms, but none seem to have an opinion on how they feel about being in Mississippi in the first place."

In the background, Stuart saw four ponchos on the highway, lying side by side. It made him sick to know that under each poncho was the body of a U.S. Marine. He had put Marines in body bags, too, and hated to be reminded of it.

Stuart moved in front of Moreland, the gun still leveled at his head.

"What do you really expect to get out of all this?" Stuart said.

Moreland said, "You don't get it, do you. You don't see the liberal dictatorship that's slowly taking over our country? Our federal government is becoming no better than the Communist government in the old Soviet Union. It's huge, inefficient, corrupt and intrusive. Government runs every aspect of our lives.

"The President—and those like him—have an agenda, one the voters never see," Moreland said. "One they can push while sounding like our protectors. They really want soft drug and crime laws because more dope dealers with guns means crime. More crime means a need for more cops—more government employees.

"More addicts means more junkie mothers and crack babies," Moreland said. "So the liberals, coming to our rescue, want welfare expanded so that more people are dependent on government. More of your tax money going to support the government and their wealth-redistribution plans. It goes on and on. They oppose a balanced-budget amendment because it takes more government to deal with the deficit. They want to legalize abortion so they can establish yet another government agency to regulate it. They don't want Americans—at least the law-abiding ones—to own guns. They'd rather have a defenseless population, so that when the drug dealers with guns come into their neighborhoods, they'll have to turn to the government for help."

Stuart lowered his pistol ever so slightly. He shook his head. "Moreland, you're paranoid and crazy."

Moreland shrugged. "Am I? Then answer this: Why are U.S.

Marines fighting in Okolona?"

Stuart couldn't answer that question because he wasn't sure himself. He gestured with his weapon. "Let's go," he said.

The old man rose slowly. As he did, Stuart saw a glimmer of silver from his right hand. Moreland raised a pistol, which, Stuart realized with a sudden chill, Moreland had held throughout the confrontation.

Reflexively, Stuart fired once. The bullet hit Moreland in the forehead, killing him. He crashed backward, toppling his chair and landing face up on the plywood floor.

Stuart sank to his knees. Where's that damn task force? He slid to the wall to his right and leaned his head against the rough plywood. For the first time in more than two days, he slept.

Stuart's eyes opened to the sight of an MP5 submachine gun muzzle pointed at his head from a few feet away, where Special Agent Bill Gautier lay prone. To Gautier's left knelt another agent, similarly armed. Stuart froze.

"ATF," Gautier said. "Freeze. You're under arrest."

"I'm Special Agent Wade Stuart of the ATF," Stuart said.

Gautier did not move.

"My badge is in my coat pocket," Stuart said.

"Remove it—slowly," Gautier said.

Stuart did so and flashed the badge. Gautier lowered his weapon. The agent to his left kept his trained on Stuart.

Gautier signaled his companion, who immediately lowered his weapon. Stuart relaxed, then stood, as did the two task force agents.

Gautier pulled a radio out of a cargo pocket in his black, military-style trousers.

"Lead One," he said into the radio, "I've got a body and Special Agent Wade Stuart in here. Contact Assistant Director Carr."

Stuart looked around the bunker a final time before ascending the ladder. He shook his head slowly, as if awakening from a bad dream. Then he climbed out.

15

Stuart watched the President on the hotel room television. He was too exhausted to react, but listened intently as the President spoke eloquently about freedom and the sacrifices that must be made by the individual for the betterment of the whole. Stuart didn't know if he was talking about the sacrifices made by the Marines killed at Okolona or the sacrifice made by Americans by allowing federal troops into their neighborhoods. He was relieved the whole thing was over, and glad that it ended with only a brief skirmish.

But he felt uneasy still.

Out there, across the country, remained hundreds of militias, all with a similar goal as Amos Moreland. And they were not intimidated by the federal government. The publicity of this case would most likely martyr Amos Moreland and the MPM, Stuart thought as he listened to Lee Ann shower in the adjacent bathroom. In that respect, he mused, he had failed in his mission. The militias would add the episode to a growing list of attacks by the federal government.

And they'll burrow even deeper into the nation's underground. The use of troops raised the ante, Stuart thought.

And listening to the President, Stuart knew there would be a next time. Hearing him say that "we must constantly be on guard against those who would deny us our freedoms and stop them by all means necessary" gave Stuart a chill.

He didn't know which he feared more, the militias or the federal government.

Lee Ann emerged from the shower in a cloud of steam, patting her hair dry with a towel. Stuart watched her hungrily as she walked to the bed, wrapped in a towel that rode up her legs with each step.

EPILOGUE

S pecial Agent Wade Stuart stepped into the conference room. He wore a well-tailored dark suit, crisp white shirt and perfectly knotted burgundy tie. He was clean-shaven and had even gotten a haircut, although his black hair was still a bit longer than most agents allowed.

Inside the room in Washington, D.C., were various luminaries of the ATF, including a representative from the Treasury Department and the interim director, Billy Simpson.

Interim Director Simpson motioned Stuart into a chair. Stuart sat at one end of the polished wooden table. The room was very quiet.

"Special Agent Stuart, thank you for coming today," Simpson said.

Stuart nodded.

"Today, as part of our after-action brief, we'd like to discuss the chronology of your investigation of the Mississippi People's Militia," Simpson said.

Not even a thank you, Stuart thought as he nodded again. He listened as Simpson read dates, times, and brief descriptions of Stuart's role in the operation. He knew what was coming.

Even though the President's spin doctors had turned the crisis into fairly favorable poll numbers, showing moderate support, inside the White House, the view prevailed that the crisis was an avoidable debacle created by the ATF.

The firing—or quitting, depending on which side you were

on—of Director Charles Norman was proof of that, at least to the White House.

Stuart knew that he would be next, to make the White House story complete. He had to be at fault, so that proof existed that the President had had no choice.

A half-smile crossed Stuart's face as Simpson rattled on at the opposite end of the table. Stuart slipped his hand inside his coat pocket and removed a small flat ID card case.

Simpson looked up. Stuart tossed his badge halfway down the length of the table. Simpson watched it spin to a stop. He looked at Stuart.

"Keep it," Stuart said, then looked at the young woman who was recording the meeting on a stenographer's pad. "I want this on the record that I quit. You're not hanging this on me, Simpson. I know what's going on here. The President needs a paper trail to support his otherwise insupportable actions. I won't be a part of it."

He stood, shoving his chair back forcefully behind him.

"What happened in Mississippi was wrong, as wrong as it could be," Stuart said. "And it set a dangerous precedent. For years, these militias have been screaming about the federal government taking away their freedom and the American dictatorship that's developing right in front of us. I, like most people, dismissed these guys as a bunch of crackpots. Until now."

Stuart glanced about the room at dumbfounded faces. He continued. "We did exactly what they said we'd do someday," he said. "And it wasn't that hard. A few speeches by a man who has done wonders to chip away at our individual rights, a man who heads the largest federal government in history, and just like that, we've got a federal force attacking American citizens."

He snapped his fingers, looked for someone to stop him, and when nobody spoke, he forged ahead. "So what's next? The precedent has been set, and that will make it that much easier the next time. And, believe me, there will be a next time. Maybe next time, we'll neutralize the militia and take away their guns. While we're there, let's take away the guns of everybody in the county, just to be sure. We don't need search warrants—we're using the military."

The room was quiet. Simpson wore a stern look as the stenographer scribbled furiously.

"Where does it end?" Stuart said. "Certainly not here. We did nothing—absolutely nothing—to eliminate the militia threat in this country. They're still out there, with all the proof they need that our government really is an evil, spreading dictatorship. How are you going to handle them? With a greater role for the post-Cold War military and eliminate ATF altogether? We only made it worse. More bad times are coming, Simpson, and all the finger-pointing in the world won't prevent it. And the most despicable part of it all is that four Marines are dead."

He hesitated and thought for a second. Then he let out a deep breath. "I won't be a part of the systematic shredding of the Constitution. I resign!" Stuart said.

He turned quickly and exited the room, leaving a disconcerted group staring at the table.

He exhaled loudly as he bounded down the steps of the Treasury Building and onto the sidewalk. He saw the idling rental car and jogged to the passenger door.

He jumped in and leaned across the seat to kiss Lee Ann.

"See? It didn't take long," he said.

She smiled, glanced over her shoulder and pulled into traffic. She craned her neck and peered through the windshield at the leaden November sky.

"Looks like the rain is about to start," she said.

Stuart looked across the capital at the bureaucrats scurrying to and from their government cubbyholes. His mind flashed to the previous autumn and a line of men firing automatic weapons on the MPM range.

"Yeah, I know," he said. "I was thinking the same thing."

MEMPHIS RIBS
Gerald Duff

Memphis Ribs is a genre-bending, hard-boiled mystery about J.W. Ragsdale, Memphis Homicide Detective, who seeks the murderer of a tourist and a local society giant during the May International Barbecue Contest and the Cotton Carnival, two events spanning Memphis society and culture.

Memphis Ribs pits the greed and arrogance of old money against the easy money of narcotics, masterfully capturing the intersection and dialect of both worlds.

"Memphis Ribs will stick to yours. It's got a detective who knows how to talk and what to do and an author who knows how to write." —*Roy Blount Jr.*

"Gerald Duff has an unerring ear for Memphis dialect." —*The Washington Post*

Available in May at your favorite bookstore.

To order a copy direct from the publisher, send your name, address, and a check or money order for $12.95 ($15.95 in Canada) for each book ordered, plus $2.00 for postage and handling payable to Salvo Press, to:

Salvo Press
61149 South Hwy 97, Suite 134
Bend, OR 97702

TREVOR SCOTT

EXTREME FACTION   0-9664520-3-8, $12.95

Jake Adams, former CIA officer and Air Force Intelligence captain, is back with a new thrilling adventure. This second installment pits Jake against some of the most idealistic terrorists ever to strap on a suicide bomb. Jake is hired by a Portland, Oregon company as a private security agent during an international agriculture conference in Odessa, Ukraine. When a world-renowned bio-chemist is murdered, Jake seeks his killer. The scientist had been the foremost authority on chemical and biological weapons, developing the most deadly agents for the former Soviet Union. Was he still secretly developing those deadly weapons? Only one man can stop the deadly plan...Jake Adams!

Available in August at your favorite bookstore.

FATAL NETWORK   0-9664520-0-3, $12.95

A gripping story of murder, espionage and suspense. A tech rep at a U.S. Air Base in Germany is missing and Jake Adams is the only one who can find him. Trying desperately to save the woman he loves, he must first keep the technology away from ruthless German and Hungarian agents.

Available now at all fine bookstores.

Praise for Trevor Scott and Fatal Network

"Fatal Network is a masterfully written, splendidly executed, superb thriller."—_The Midwest Book Review_

"This is a thriller with some real thrills, an adventure with new ideas, and an espionage drama firmly rooted in the convoluted realities of modern Europe."—_Statesman Journal_, Salem, Oregon

"A roller coaster ride of murder, espionage and intrigue."
                    —**David Hagberg**, bestselling author of _High Flight_